"Mad at me?" Case asked lightly, his fingers caressing the sensitive skin of her arm.

"Why should I be? You've just made me the latest item on the hospital grapevine!" Sharla tried to pull away, but he wouldn't release her. "By tomorrow everyone will think we're having a torrid affair."

The elevator arrived and Case pulled her inside. "They'll be right."

"No!" Her voice was shaky. "I absolutely refuse. The hot clinch in the elevator is such a staple in every hospital romance that it's become a ridiculous cliché."

His mouth twitched in amusement, but a flame was burning in his blue eyes. "You're trembling, Sharla. You want it as much as I do."

"I don't." She took a step backward and bumped into the wall of the elevator. Case advanced deliberately, leaning forward until she could feel the hardness of his muscular thighs against her softness.

Sharla put her hands on his chest, ostensibly to shove him away. But her plans went awry. "No," she protested, even as her arms were winding around his neck to pull him closer. "It's not fair," she murmured as his lips brushed hers in a series of feather-light caresses.

"What isn't fair, sweet?" Case whispered, pulling her tighter against him.

"That you should feel so good," she said breathlessly. "That you should taste so good. . . ."

WHAT ARE *LOVESWEPT* ROMANCES?

They are stories of true romance and touching emotion. We believe those two very important ingredients are constants in our highly sensual and very believable stories in the *LOVESWEPT* line. Our goal is to give you, the reader, stories of consistently high quality that may sometimes make you laugh, sometimes make you cry, but are always fresh and creative and contain many delightful surprises within their pages.

Most romance fans read an enormous number of books. Those they truly love, they keep. Others may be traded with friends and soon forgotten. We hope that each *LOVESWEPT* romance will be a treasure—a "keeper." We will always try to publish

*LOVE STORIES YOU'LL NEVER FORGET
BY AUTHORS YOU'LL ALWAYS REMEMBER*

The Editors

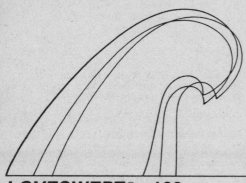

LOVESWEPT® • 160

Barbara Boswell
Bedside Manners

 BANTAM BOOKS
·TORONTO · NEW YORK · LONDON · SYDNEY · AUCKLAND

BEDSIDE MANNERS

A Bantam Book / October 1986

If you would be interested in receiving protective vinyl
covers for your Loveswept books, please write to this address
for information:

Loveswept
Bantam Books
P.O. Box 985
Hicksville, NY 11802

ISBN 0-553-21782-8

Published simultaneously in the United States and Canada

PRINTED IN THE UNITED STATES OF AMERICA

O   0 9 8 7 6 5 4 3 2 1

One

Case saw her the moment he entered the hospital conference room, which had been decorated for the occasion with balloons and crepe paper streamers. She held a cup of punch and sipped from it as she laughed and nodded and talked to the group of interns and nurses surrounding her.

Her eyes were alive with intelligence and humor, her expression alert and animated. She seemed to radiate warmth and magnetism. Case found her as fascinating to observe as he had the first time he'd seen her, last month in the Administrator of Finance's office. Then he'd watched her charm the appropriations officer into giving the hospital's Intensive Care Nursery the go-ahead to purchase some brand-new and ultraexpensive womb-simulating Isolettes.

He remembered her name, of course. Sharla Shakarian. A name memorable in its own right, he'd thought upon hearing it. She was a neo-natologist, a pediatrician who specialized in the care of sick infants in their first critical months of life. Premature babies and babies born with physical anomalies comprised the neonatologist's practice.

Case continued to assess her. She was about five feet five in her low-heeled shoes, but her slender, small-boned frame made her seem delicately petite. The clothes she was wearing were tailored and serviceable—flared gray skirt, pale pink blouse, and starched white coat—but seemed to heighten her softly rounded curves.

Her face was dominated by large, wide-set eyes, the darkest he'd ever seen, the color of ebony ink. Though her features were too uneven to classify her as beautiful, her wide, generous mouth, turned-up nose, and firm little chin gave her an appeal that Case found far more interesting than classic beauty.

He watched her tuck a strand of her silky, jet-black hair behind her ear. She wore it in a page boy that framed her face and hung slightly below her chin. Her dark, thick bangs accentuated her huge eyes—which suddenly snapped up and connected with his.

Case didn't look away. He held her gaze, seeing her nod to the intern on her left as she maintained the eye contact between them. His lips curved into a slow smile. She wasn't about to be the first to look away, he thought. And neither was he. Enjoying the silent duel, he met the challenge in her eyes.

"Dr. Flynn!"

The sound of his name and a firm hand on his arm forced him to break their locked gaze. A surprising surge of annoyance shot through him, but he managed to conceal it as he turned to the older woman now clutching his arm.

"How nice of you to come, Dr. Flynn," the woman exclaimed, and Case smiled at her, all traces of his momentary irritation erased. He genuinely liked Marge Deaver, and respected her too.

"I wanted to pay my respects to the best Director of Nursing this hospital's ever had, Marge," he said sincerely. "None of us in ST will ever forget the times you went down to the wire for our nurses."

"I went down to the wire for all my nurses," Marge corrected him, and Case grinned.

"That's right, Marge!" He knew very well that Marge Deaver had a special relationship with the nurses in the hospital's Shock/Trauma Unit, where he was a thoracic surgeon. And that she categorically denied any such thing.

"So, what's your successor like?" he asked. Nursing administration on the whole didn't interest him, but he knew the nurses on his staff were worried that the new Director of Nursing wouldn't be as supportive as Margery Deaver. And Case made it a point to keep his nurses happy.

"You'll be thrilled to know," Marge said, "that the new director has a background as an emergency care supervisor and is very interested in the Shock/Trauma Unit. She also has a vital interest in the Intensive Care Nursery. Her cousin is a neonatologist there."

Case raised his brows. "No kidding?"

"No kidding. There's Clare Maridian now." Marge nodded toward a slim, dark-haired woman, somewhere in her mid-forties, who had just slipped her arm around . . . Sharla Shakarian? "Dr. Shakarian is her first cousin. I'm told they're quite close."

"Terrific," Case said dryly. "Dr. Shakarian has the Administrator of Finance wrapped around her little finger and now she's got the Director of Nursing in her pocket. Schroeder is going to love it." Jake Schroeder was the head of the Shock/Trauma Unit and quite territorial about the unit's favored position among the hospital's administrative hierarchy. He wouldn't want to share that privileged position with any other unit, not even the Intensive Care Nursery for sick newborns and premature babies. And, in truth, neither would Case.

Two nurses approached Marge Deaver for a teary farewell. Case drifted toward the refreshment table, where he was handed a cup of red punch with pink sherbert melting in it. His gaze seemed to veer automatically to the section of the room where Sharla Shakarian was holding court. She and the newly appointed Director of Nursing had their arms around each other's waists and were smiling at a group of student nurses who'd encircled them.

As he gazed at them, Sharla glanced up and met his eyes again. She raised her brows. Case raised his. Once again, she refused to break the gaze, and this time Case was determined not to be the first to look away. The student nurses scurried off, and the new Director of Nursing's attention was claimed by another well-wisher. For one long moment Case and Sharla stood and stared at each other across the crowded, noisy room.

Still holding Casey Flynn's gaze, Sharla watched him cross the room toward her, his long-legged stride determined and masculinely aggressive. The loose-fitting green surgical scrub suit he wore accentuated his strong and rangy masculine frame. He was tall, at least an inch or two over six feet, and the proverbial "dark and handsome" could be applied to him as well. His thick shock of black hair was silver-tipped at his temples, and his eyes, a unique shade of blue so light it could almost be described as the color of water, were fringed by thick lashes.

He certainly knew how to make those beautiful eyes work for him, Sharla thought with amusement. He was quite skilled in the art of eye contact, as she'd discovered during the two rounds he'd engaged her in this afternoon.

He was at her side now, and she had to look up to maintain their locked gaze. Still, she did not avert her eyes. "Hello, Dr. Flynn." She smiled at him.

Case felt a distinct jolt as he continued to stare down at her. Her smile packed an incredible wallop. No wonder the Intensive Care Nursery chief had sent her to weasel the Isolettes out of the tight-fisted finance officer. When she smiled in that certain way, with her head cocked a little and her lashes sweeping over her big, velvet-black eyes, it would be damn difficult to say no to whatever she asked.

"You . . . know who I am?" he said. That surprised him. They hadn't been introduced during the brief meeting that day in the administrator's office, which had been crowded-to-overflowing with other people.

"I know who you are," she said. "Your reputation precedes you, Dr. Flynn."

Case blinked. She had a deep dimple in her right cheek. Her dark eyes were brimming with amusement. And he liked her voice. It was naturally husky and well modulated. She seemed to exude energy and brightness. He couldn't take his gaze from her.

He cleared his throat. "Which reputation is that?" he asked modestly, knowing full well that he was renowned as a premier trauma surgeon. *The Washingtonian* had done an in-depth article on the Hospital Center's Shock/Trauma Unit, and he and his skills had been prominently featured. He'd made fund-raising appearances on local TV and radio talk shows as well.

"Your reputation as a bona fide heartthrob," Sharla said with a grin, totally taking him aback. "Clare and I just listened to a gaggle of student nurses sighing over 'that gorgeous hunk, Dr. Flynn.' It seems you could take your pick of any one of them in this room."

"Student nurses?" Case groaned. "Give me a break! They're children. And my tastes don't run to little girls."

"That's fortunate. Because from the tales I've heard, you're no match for any little girl. Even the most sophisticated ladies are supposedly at risk with you."

Case's jaw tightened and his dark brows drew together. Sharla Shakarian was unexpectedly cheeky. And he wasn't accustomed to such bluntness, especially from a woman. "I don't care to discuss my personal life," he said forbiddingly.

"No?" She chuckled, undaunted. "Then you must be the only one in the Hospital Center who doesn't. Your personal life seems to be the favorite topic of everyone else around here."

"Dr. Shakarian," he began in the icily controlled tone which caused his staff to tread lightly, "I—"

"You know who I am?" she interrupted him with his own words.

"Yes, I do. And you—"

"Then why the cute little eye games?" she interrupted him again, staring at him in surprise. "And why did you bother coming over to talk to me if you know I'm not a nurse?"

Case felt a surge of heat stain his neck and spread slowly upward. *Cute little eye games*? And what about that little crack alluding to his preference for nurses? He'd been insulted! he fumed indignantly. He should simply turn and walk away from her. But he didn't. Instead he stayed put and glowered at her. "Are you always this . . . brash, Dr. Shakarian?"

"Oh, always," she assured him. "So I've finally met the notorious Dr. Flynn. I've seen you in the cafeteria a few times, and your prowess, of course, is legendary." She laughed at his astonished expression.

He really was a marvelous-looking man, she thought, with those Black Irish looks and his trim athlete's body. When he'd begun his seductive eye contact today, she'd mischievously decided to play along with him, certain that he'd mistaken her for a nurse. It was common knowledge that Case Flynn never got involved with women doctors, although a number had certainly been willing. He kept his relationships with female physicians strictly and carefully professional. "How does it feel to be a Hospital Center legend in your own time, doctor?" she asked.

Case knew she was *not* referring to his legendary

prowess as a trauma surgeon. She was laughing at him! He stared at her, not at all sure how to take her. He could count on one hand the times that he'd been at a loss for words around a woman. This was definitely one of them—the others had occurred back in junior high school. "Dr. Shakarian, are you implying that I've acquired a reputation as something of a—a—"

"Nurse-chaser?" she supplied helpfully. "I'll say you have! Do you know that our head nurse in the Intensive Care Nursery feels obligated to warn every young, single nurse we get about the irresistible but dangerous Dr. Flynn? Rumor has it you've done more damage to hearts than can be found in the Cardiac Care Unit."

"You make me sound like some kind of a—a Casanova in a scrub suit!" Case was appalled. And incensed. "I assure you it's not true!"

He was more than a little shocked by her frankness. No woman had ever spoken to him like this. His relations with his physician colleagues were impeccably correct. And the nurses on his team idolized him, while the nurses elsewhere . . . He felt a flush slowly suffuse his cheeks. The nurses elsewhere were either deferential—if they were old or married; or responded eagerly to his sexual overtures—if they were pretty, young, and single. He shifted uncomfortably under Sharla's steady, dark-eyed gaze. "It's not true," he repeated somewhat lamely.

"Not true?" She looked disappointed. "You mean all those great stories I've heard are exaggerations or outright lies?" She shrugged and heaved a sigh. "What a revelation! Next you'll be telling me not to believe everything I read in the *National Enquirer*."

Case stared at her. Her black eyes were sparkling with humor and her mouth was quivering with suppressed laughter. "You're a brat!" he exclaimed, for in that moment she reminded him of his kid sister, who used to tease him gleefully, just to see if she could get a rise out of him.

Sharla shook her head. "No, I'm Armenian. We're quite frank and outspoken, you see. Unlike you Irish, who can talk glibly for hours and never manage to get to the point."

"No fair drawing on ethnic stereotypes. My family hasn't been in Ireland for the last hundred years." He laughed suddenly. "I'm a full-blooded American who can talk glibly for hours and never manage to get to the point."

He was incredibly attractive when he laughed like that, Sharla thought as her pulses skipped a beat. Who was she kidding? He was incredibly attractive when he was frowning or serious or totally deadpan. She suspected he would look good even with a runny nose and a head cold!

Her eyes connected with his again and they smiled at each other. There was a brief fluttering in her stomach and she fought the urge to lower her eyes demurely. That would be a tactical error. She instinctively knew that a woman had to hold her own against a man like Casey Flynn or risk total subjugation by him.

"So you're Armenian?" he said. She intrigued him, he grudgingly admitted to himself, much more than he cared to acknowledge. "How many generations removed from the old country? Wherever that is," he added with a grin.

"You Irish-Americans have no sense of geography," she complained. "As any Armenian-American can tell you, Armenia is now part of the Soviet Union, except the part that the Turks and the Iranians have. My grandparents came to America when they were in their teens. They were the only members of their families to survive the Armenian deportation by the Turks during World War One." She gazed into space, remembering her grandparents' harrowing, heartbreaking tales. "The others all died on the death march."

Her voice trembled a little and the light had gone

out of her eyes. She spoke as if it were a recent trag-edy, Case thought. He felt compelled to try to make her smile again. "I remember my grandmother talking about the starving Armenians. Somehow she always brought them up whenever my sister and I refused to eat the abysmal corned beef and cabbage she'd put in front of us."

His anecdote did not achieve the effect he'd hoped for. Sharla didn't smile; her expression grew even bleaker. Her thoughts were clearly still with her unfortunate antecedents. "It was a terrible period in our history. All that suffering, all those lives lost . . ."

She was so serious, her ebony eyes so large and sad, that Case was puzzled, oddly touched, yet amused all at the same time. He'd never been one to get emotional over any issue, let alone a remote historical one. But Sharla seemed to take the events in a faraway country half a century ago to heart.

"What's past is past, Sharla. You don't expect me to get upset over the Irish potato famine, I hope," he couldn't resist saying. "That's what drove the Flynns out of Mother Ireland all those years ago." He cupped her chin lightly and tilted it upward with his thumb.

The light touch of his fingers on the creamy soft-ness of her skin sent a totally unexpected blaze of heat through them both. Sharla's first instinct was to jump away; Case's was to pull her against him. Neither of them moved. For one long moment they stood stock-still, ink-black eyes staring into water-blue ones.

And then Sharla took a small step backward. Case's hand dropped to his side. He swallowed reflexively. Good Lord, what had happened to him? he wondered. For a few seconds there he'd felt as if he'd been struck by a lightning bolt. And he'd merely touched her! He cleared his throat, attempting to gather his shattered wits about him. "Uh, what were we talking about?"

Sharla seemed equally dazed. "The Irish potato famine." She gave her head a shake as if to clear it. The man was dangerous, all right, she thought. He'd merely touched her and she'd been completely immobilized. When had anyone's touch ever affected her that way?

"Ah, yes." Case had regained his cool. "Do you realize that this is the first and only time I've ever discussed the Irish potato famine and the starving Armenians with a woman?"

"I would guess it's the first and only time you've ever discussed the Irish potato famine and the starving Armenians with *anyone*," she said dryly. She, too, had regained her composure.

"You missed your cue, Sharla." He leaned a little closer, his blue gaze traveling lazily over her, his voice and stance frankly seductive. "You're supposed to ask, 'What do you usually discuss with a woman, Case?' "

Sharla felt a flash of irritation. "Oh, I don't have to ask, I *know*." He was so smooth, such an accomplished flirt. The body language, the low, lilting voice, those seductive blue eyes. And she had the strongest, strangest feeling that it was all a sham. The friendly, devilish flirt was merely a mask, and the real man was hidden deep within, behind an unreachable wall of reserve.

"You know?" he asked. He seemed to tower over her. The way he was standing, the way he was looking at her made her feel small and feminine, in direct contrast to his big, masculine frame. His eyes bored into hers; it was as if they were the only two people in the room—in the world!

"Yes." Sharla was breathless, and it annoyed her. The man's every move was so practiced, doubtlessly honed to perfection down through the years! She knew it and was still affected by him. She could feel herself flushing and her heart beginning to race.

With some effort, she tried to control her runaway response. "I'm fairly certain that there are only two subjects in the world that you freely discuss, Dr. Flynn. Sex and medicine. The first is restricted to your *amours*, the second to your colleagues." She stared up at him defiantly.

"You're a feisty little thing, aren't you, Sharla?" A slow, sexy grin tilted the corners of his lips. "And you're small and soft and irresistibly feminine." He watched the telltale pulse beat at the base of her throat begin to throb, and he knew he was getting to her. It pleased him. She'd managed to throw him off balance for a while there. Now he was recouping lost ground.

His voice lowered intimately. "If we weren't standing in the middle of a reception for the outgoing and incoming Directors of Nursing, I'd take you in my arms and make you open your mouth for me, little one. And then I'd—"

"You're getting confused, Flynn," she interrupted. She *had* to interrupt. His words were making her weak and hot and . . . That satisfied male gleam in his eye brought her fighting instincts to the fore. "That's the sexy talk you reserve for your nurse conquests. I'm a fellow physician, remember? You're programmed to talk medicine to me. "So." Her dark eyes flashed black fire. "What's your opinion of the Jarvik-7 heart? Do you see it as a stopgap measure or as an end in itself?"

Case gaped at her. Something had definitely gone wrong here. Seconds ago she'd been aroused and ready to melt for him, and now she was briskly discussing the Jarvik-7 artificial heart?

"Mmm-hmm, you've been thrown off the track, Dr. Flynn," she said succinctly. "You see, there's a course offered to female medical students that isn't yet available in the nursing schools. It's called Dealing With the Physician As Wolf 101. I got an *A* in it. I think I could even teach it. That's why your line didn't elicit its customary successful response from me."

Case tried to come back with some suitable comment. His ego told him he should be angry with her. She seemed to delight in besting him at his own game. But he simply couldn't rouse any macho outrage. He thought she was funny. She was quick and sharp-tongued and he had two sisters who were a lot like her, both of whom he appreciated very much. She interested him in a way that most women did not.

"Has the silver-tongued Dr. Flynn been rendered speechless?" she asked, humor dancing in her black eyes. "This must be a historical first."

She was baiting him and he found it impossible to resist nibbling a little. "I concede this round to you, you little Armenian spitfire." His gaze swept over her daintily rounded figure. "Which only means I'm absolutely determined to win the next."

Before Sharla could reply, both she and Case were diverted by an excited, girlish voice calling her name. "Sharla! Oh, Sharla, hi!"

Case was certain that the pretty, dark-haired, dark-eyed young nurse who rushed up to Sharla was another relative. The resemblance was unmistakable. "Hi, Beth." Sharla greeted her warmly. "Have you seen Clare yet?"

"Not yet. Oh, isn't it exciting, Sharla? Our Clare, the Director of Nursing!" Beth exclaimed enthusiastically. "Everyone in the family is so proud!"

Case, ignored up to this point, cleared his throat to get their attention. He wasn't accustomed to being ignored. The younger girl's reaction was almost comical. She stared at Case, her eyes wide, her mouth agape.

Sharla glanced from Beth to Case, then drew in her breath sharply. "Beth, this is Casey Flynn. Dr. Flynn, my cousin, Beth Shakarian."

Case took Beth's hand and smiled down at her. "Hello, Beth."

"H-hi," she breathed.

"You must be new here at the hospital, Beth." Case continued to smile and to hold her hand in his. "I'd remember if I'd seen *you* before."

"I—I've been here two weeks," Beth said quickly.

"I'm working in labor and delivery." Her eyes flicked briefly to Sharla. "I'm staying with Sharla until I find an apartment and a roommate of my own."

"Are there any more Shakarian cousins on the staff here?" Case asked, smiling a smile that sent Beth reeling, and made Sharla long to wipe it off— with her fists! It was such a practiced smile, the smile of a world-class smooth operator. Sharla knew it was his stock-in-trade smile for his standard nurse seductions.

"Our cousin Tim is a pharmacist here," she said, inserting herself into the conversation, her voice brisk. "And we have two cousins in med school who affiliate here."

"And our cousin Toni is considering coming in as a consulting psychologist in the mental health clinic," Beth added eagerly. "She has a private practice in Maryland."

"A virtual Armenian takeover!" Case said, smiling.

Sharla did not return the smile. She glanced pointedly at her watch. "Beth, you'd better go on over and talk to Clare, honey. You don't want to be gone from the labor and delivery suite too long."

Beth nodded grudgingly. "Good-bye, Dr. Flynn."

"Case," he corrected her, and smiled again. "Good-bye, Beth. It's been a pleasure meeting you. I'll see you again, I'm sure."

Sharla was afraid Beth was going to swoon on the spot. She watched her young cousin float across the crowded room, then turned on Casey Flynn. "Over my dead body, Flynn."

"What do you mean?"

"Leave my little cousin alone!"

He was instantly annoyed. "For Pete's sake, Sharla, I was simply being polite."

"Polite, ha! First you hit her with that knock-'em-dead smile of yours and then you follow it up with the soft bedroom voice." Her onyx eyes were intense. "Beth is only twenty-one, and she's very sweet and very trusting and *very* naive. She's led a sheltered life in Racine and—"

"Racine? Where on earth is that?"

"You really are pitiful in geography, Flynn. Racine, Wisconsin. It's where our whole family is from. There's a sizable Armenian population there and it's where my grandparents ended up when they emigrated in 1919." She squared her shoulders and pinned him with a stern glare. "I promised Bethy's parents, my uncle Michael and aunt Jean, that I'd keep an eye on her here in Washington. And I intend to do so. It's her first time away from home."

"And you're implying that a snake like me will pounce on a sweet, naive young thing like her and gobble her up for breakfast?"

"Dare I say it? If the skin fits . . ."

"Your sweet little cousin doesn't interest me, Dr. Shakarian," Case said coolly. "She's almost twenty years younger than I am. I told you that little girls hold no appeal for me. Dammit, what kind of stories have you heard that've given you such a low opinion of me, anyway?"

Perhaps he'd meant it as a rhetorical question, but Sharla chose to give him an answer. "I've been told that you regard your own team of nurses as sacrosanct, but that it's always open season on nurses in any other department. You've worked your way through the med-surg floors, and the clinics, and pediatrics, and OB, and the OR and the ER and—"

"If I were as active as the gossipmongers say, when would I possibly have time to practice medicine?"

"I've wondered about that," Sharla said slowly.

"You work in a high-pressure, high-risk critical care unit too. Don't you think it's possible that maybe, *just maybe*, the stories are exaggerated? You know how time-consuming and energy-draining our line of work is."

"Well . . ." A reluctant smile slowly played across her face. "*Just maybe*, I suppose."

"It's most kind of the good doctor to toss me a few crumbs." Case felt his anger draining as quickly as it had come. It was impossible for him to stay annoyed with her when she smiled.

What was it about her that affected him so? he wondered. Her cousin Beth was prettier and younger, and gazed at him with a hero worship he knew he would never see in Sharla Shakarian's eyes. And Sharla had been right to be concerned about his effect on her young cousin. Normally, the pretty little nurse would've been just his type, and he would have pursued her until he effortlessly won her. But not within the last year, he conceded, and had to suppress a sigh. As his fortieth birthday had approached, he'd found himself afflicted with a whopping case of ennui, which he utterly refused to call a mid-life crisis. He would not, he *could* not be so boringly predictable, he'd assured himself.

"Well?" Sharla interrupted his reverie. She was staring up at him, her eyes challenging. "Do I have your word that you'll keep away from Beth?"

He arched his brows. "Suppose I decide to pursue you instead?"

Her heart jumped. Sharla was liked at her schoolgirl response and irritated that Case had effectively elicited it. "That's hardly likely, Dr. Flynn. Your preferences run to nurses. Lots and lots of them."

Damn, why did he feel the need to justify himself to her? He should tell her to go dunk her head in the punch bowl. But he didn't. "I've had affairs, perhaps more than my fair share, but I'm forty years old, Sharla. I'm neither gay nor asexual. Of course there have been women in my life. And if they've all been nurses, it's probably because I spend almost all my time in the hospital. Who else am I going to meet?"

"There *is* an alternative to a never-ending string

of affairs," she pointed out, holding her own under his ice-water stare. "One that most men of forty have tried at least once. It's an age-old institution that's still alive and well today. It's called marriage."

He laughed. "Yeah, I've heard of it. My folks tried it—what a disaster! I decided in grade school that it wasn't for me."

"Oh, come on, Flynn, that doesn't wash! If I lived my life based on my grade-school decisions, I'd alternate weekly between being a fireman and a ballerina."

"I've never found any reason to change my mind about marriage," he said in a voice so serious that Sharla knew he wasn't kidding, joking, or teasing. "My sister and I have often said that we'd rather be dead than be married. We both mean it."

"Oh." There didn't seem to be much else to say. He really did mean it, Sharla thought, and she felt absurdly, inexorably sad for him. What set of circumstances had led him to such a depressing decision?

"I suppose you're a firm believer in the blessed state of holy matrimony?" Case's voice was caustic.

"I am." She lifted her head and met his gaze unflinchingly. "My grandparents have been married sixty-six years, my parents thirty-five. And all my aunts and uncles have had long, successful marriages too."

"Yeah, well . . ." He shrugged. "Maybe you Armenians go in for that sort of thing, but I don't."

"Yes, you'd rather be in a cemetery than married."

"You've got it, baby."

There was something about his masculine smirk that challenged her. She looked straight into his mocking blue eyes. "I have a prediction to make, Dr. Flynn."

"A prediction? Are you Armenians soothsayers too?"

"I predict that someday you'll fall madly in love with some cute little nurse and totally reverse your better-dead-than-wed attitude. You'll chase her the whole way to the altar and become a devoted husband and father who bores everyone with tales of his everloving little family."

He laughed shortly. "I hope you're better at practicing medicine than you are at making predictions, Dr. Shakarian. Because what you said is never, *ever* going to happen."

Sharla's electronic beeper went off at that precise moment. "I guess it's time for me to put away my crystal ball and put on my stethoscope. Good-bye, Case. It's been fun talking to you." She flashed him a farewell smile and slipped quickly from the room.

Case stared after her. Her smile had the strangest effect on him; it left him feeling dazzled. And her eyes! As shining and sparkling as polished black diamonds. She'd called him Case when she'd said good-bye; not Flynn or Dr. Flynn, but Case. It was the first time she'd said his name and he liked the sound of it in that sexy, husky voice of hers.

It's been fun talking to you. Her words played back in his head. She was right, it had been fun. His interactions with the female sex were invariably serious, dealing with either medicine or sex.

His gaze drifted to the newly appointed Director of Nursing, Clare Maridian, who was talking to the young Beth Shakarian. Case stared at the two of them for a long moment. They were slender and dark and pretty, yet they seemed to him merely pale imitations of the real thing. The real thing being their cousin, Dr. Sharla Shakarian.

Two

He was tired, Case admitted to himself as he stepped into the elevator. And *very* hungry. He'd just been cheerfully ejected from the Shock/Trauma Unit by the director and the evening charge nurse.

"You've been here for the past eighteen hours straight, Case!" Monica Cassis had said. "Go home, have a decent meal, and get some sleep."

"And don't show your face around here until at least nine o'clock tomorrow morning," Jake Schroeder had seconded firmly.

"Seven," Case had argued.

"Eight!" Monica and Jake had chorused together.

Case had grinned and walked off. But though he was tired and hungry, the thought of his quiet apartment and refrigerator stocked with frozen dinners was not a particularly appealing one. He felt wired, crackling with a tension he knew must be dispelled before he could ever hope to sleep.

He got off the elevator and stopped in front of an arrow directing people to the left and around the corner to the Intensive Care Nursery. Case blinked. What on earth was he doing *here*? He must be operating on automatic pilot or something. A picture of Sharla Shakarian flashed before his mind's eye. He'd found himself thinking of her too many times since their meeting two days ago. And now he'd been subliminally driven to the floor where she worked!

He ought to turn around and go home. There was no reason for him to be here; it made no sense at all. It was past six o'clock. Sharla probably would be gone already, even if he'd wanted to see her. Which, of course, he did not!

The curtains inside the large glass window of the Intensive Care Nursery were open. Case stared at the rows of Isolettes and warming tables inside. It looked like a science fiction laboratory. Monitoring machines were stacked on top of each other, digital numbers and lights flashing. The tiny patients were under radiant heat lights and blue lights, and connected to the machines and hanging IV bottles by a bewildering maze of tubes and hoses.

Poor babies, he thought as he stared at the wizened little creatures. Born too soon and too small. Now technology had to do what should have happened safely and naturally in their mothers' wombs.

And then he saw her. His heart kicked into an incredible rate of speed. Sharla was in the back of the nursery, talking to a tall, blond doctor who was gowned and masked, just as she was. They were both hovering over a warming table which held a tiny, dusky-red naked infant.

"Flynn. Casey Flynn." A short, rotund, balding doctor came to stand beside him. "I just read an article by you in *The New England Journal of Medicine.*" The older man beamed. "Excellent article—about cardiovascular damage in blunt force chest injuries." He extended his hand. "I'm Mel Chehovitz."

Case shook hands. He knew the name. "Chief of Pediatrics, right?"

Mel Chehovitz smiled and nodded, pleased with the recognition.

"So you're head of this outfit." Case nodded toward the nursery. Sharla's boss. The one who'd sent her to the Administrator of Finance to finagle the funds for the nursery equipment they'd wanted.

"It's my pride and joy," Mel said. "Come in and have a look around, Dr. Flynn," he invited enthusiastically. "We're doing things here that we never even dreamed of ten years ago."

"Case," Case said. "I'd like to see the nursery."

Both men donned long white gowns and masks before entering the nursery proper. Mel led Case over to the warming table where Sharla and the blond doctor stood. The young doctor was trying to draw blood from the infant's tiny arm, which was no larger than an adult's finger. Twice he tried to insert the needle into a vein, and he failed both times. The baby grimaced in pain and kicked its pencil-thin legs, but made no sound. The tube in her throat prevented her from crying aloud.

Case winced. He'd never seen a human being that small. Although he felt impatient with the perspiring young doctor, he also sympathized with his plight. The infant's veins had to be minuscule. Trying to hit one would be akin to finding the proverbial needle in the haystack.

"This is Brian Cranston," Mel said, "one of our first-year residents. And Sharla Shakarian, who's on staff." Brian looked up and nodded; Sharla never acknowledged their presence. Her entire concentration was focused on the baby.

"It's okay, Little Bit," she said. "It's all right. Just one more time, I promise." She spoke softly, reassuringly, as if the tiny girl could actually understand her. "Get me a clean needle and vial, Brian," she ordered briskly, and the resident jumped to do her bidding. Within a minute she had inserted the needle, drawn the blood sample, and handed it to a nearby nurse.

"Well done, Sharla!" Mel exclaimed. He turned his attention to the younger man. "She has an extraordinary talent for never missing, right, Brian? Did you see how she did it?"

Sharla looked up from the baby for the first time. Her gauze mask highlighted the luminous beauty of her huge ebony eyes, which widened at the sight of Case. He felt the now familiar jolt of sexual electricity he was beginning to associate with the thought or sight of her.

"This is Little Bit," she said, touching the infant's tiny hand. "She was five hundred grams at birth, just one ounce over one pound, the smallest baby we've ever had make it. She's six weeks old now and doing remarkably well."

"Six weeks?" Case dragged his gaze from Sharla to stare incredulously at the infant. "My younger sister had a baby a month ago, and he looks like a linebacker for the Chicago Bears compared to this little thing. His birth weight was nine pounds."

Mel chuckled. "If we ever got a nine-pound baby in here, we'd hand him a stethoscope and a white gown and put him to work."

The four doctors stepped into a small office adjoining the nursery and removed their masks. A stocky, gray-haired nurse was sitting at the desk, initialing charts.

"Damn, you're good, Sharla," Brian Cranston said with wistful admiration. "Your fingers move like lightning and you never screw up."

"Accuracy and precision. That's what you have to strive for," Mel said. "You mustn't compare yourself with Sharla, Brian. She's incredibly gifted," he added as consolation.

"You'd better watch the extravagant compliments, Mel," Sharla said lightly. "I might get a swelled head. And keep in mind that you didn't know me as a first-year resident. I couldn't have hit that vein then either, Brian."

. She glanced at Case and found him watching her. Was he a friend of Mel's? she wondered. She could think of no other reason for him to be here. But she was already physically reacting to his presence. Her pulses were beginning to race and there was a sharp surge of warmth deep in her abdomen. She felt his gaze focus on her mouth, and her lips began to tingle as if he had touched her with his fingers, with his lips . . .

"Sharla and I already know each other," Case said, not looking away from her. "In fact, I'm here to see if she's ready to go off duty. We have a dinner date tonight."

Everyone stared at Sharla. To her absolute horror, she felt her cheeks begin to grow warm. Why, she was blushing like a schoolgirl, something she hadn't done since she *was* a schoolgirl! She was mortified.

"You never mentioned you had a date with Dr. Flynn tonight, Sharla," exclaimed the nurse whose name pin said Evelyn Foster.

"Look, Evelyn, she's blushing." Brian grinned conspiratorially at the nurse. "Hey, Sharla, trying to keep secrets from the old gang, huh? Imagine, having a hot date and not spreading the word!"

"I'm sure you two will take care of that," Sharla grumbled. She looked balefully at Case. "Are you going to tell them that this date of ours is strictly a figment of your imagination, or shall I?"

"Didn't I ask you out the other day?" He snapped his fingers. "It must have slipped my mind. Oh, well, as long as I'm here, would you care to have dinner with me tonight, Sharla?"

She opened her mouth to speak, but Evelyn beat her to it. "Yes, Dr. Flynn, she would love to have dinner with you."

"Evelyn!" Sharla howled. She'd had every intention of refusing his glibly worded invitation.

"I'm with Evelyn," Brian said. "Sharla goes with Dr. Flynn. Nobody should celebrate the big Three-Oh by themselves."

"That's right!" Mel slapped his palm to his forehead. "Tomorrow is Sharla's birthday!"

"It is?" Case studied Sharla's flushed face. The soft pink color was incredibly becoming. "You're going to be thirty tomorrow?"

"Why don't you all just rent a billboard and plaster it up for all of Washington to read?" Sharla said. "Can't a person turn thirty in private around here?"

"Just thirty years old and she's already a board certified neonatologist," Mel said admiringly. "Sharla's something of a prodigy, Dr. Flynn. Graduated from high school at sixteen, from med school at twenty-three. Finished her five-year pediatric-neonatology residency at twenty-eight. We're damn lucky to have her on our staff."

"I'm impressed," Case drawled. Actually, he was. He'd graduated from medical school at the age of twenty-six.

"As well you should be," said Mel. Smiling with the benevolence of a matchmaking uncle, he put one arm around Sharla and the other around Case and walked them to the supply room adjacent to the nursery. "Sharla is finished here for the night, so you two may as well be on your way. Have a good dinner."

"We'll expect a full report tomorrow," Evelyn called, chortling with unsuppressed glee.

Sharla pulled off her white gown, dumped it into a laundry hamper, and fled into the corridor while Case was removing his gown. He caught up with her at the elevators. His big hand fastened around her upper arm and Sharla felt a tremor run through her.

"Mad at me?" Case asked blithely. His fingers began to knead the firm muscle of her arm, and she felt the effects of his touch through her aquamarine blouse right down to the sensitive skin beneath.

"Mad at you? Why should I be? You've just made me the current hot topic of gossip around here. I just *love* being the latest item on the hospital grapevine!" She tried to pull away from him, but he didn't release her. "Dammit, Case, by tomorrow everyone in the department will think we're having a torrid affair."

The elevator arrived, empty, and Case pulled her into it. "They'll be right," he said softly.

The doors snapped shut. He smiled down at her, tightening his grip on her arm as he slowly drew her toward him.

"No!" Her voice was shaky, her lips suddenly dry. "I absolutely refuse to be a party to this. The hot clinch in the hospital elevator is such a staple in the old nurse-and-doctor romances that it's become a ridiculous cliché. These days you won't even find a scene like this on *General Hospital*."

His mouth twitched with suppressed amusement, but a flame was burning in his blue eyes. "You're trembling, Sharla. You want it as much as I do."

She took a step backward. "I don't!" Another step. Her back touched the steel wall of the elevator.

"No?" He advanced deliberately, placing his palms flat against the wall on either side of her head, effectively enclosing her. His gaze roamed lazily over her.

Sharla put her hands on his chest, ostensibly to shove him away. But her plans went somewhat awry. Once she felt the hard strength of him beneath her fingers, sensual chaos took over, making her forget everything but the warmth radiating from him. His heady male scent filled her nostrils, drugging her senses. He was close, so close, and as his head lowered to hers she felt her eyelids grow heavy and her limbs become languorous. Her fingers gripped his blue cotton shirt and she hung on to him, her knees so shaky that she feared she might fall.

He leaned forward, letting her feel the unyielding hardness of his muscular thighs against her complementing softness. Her whole body was one heated throb. His lips brushed hers in a series of feather-light caresses, back and forth, over and over, until she was desperate for the hard, hungry pressure of his mouth.

"No," she protested, even as her arms were winding around his neck to pull him closer. "It's not fair." She tilted her head back, allowing him greater access to her long, slender neck.

He nibbled with his teeth, then laved with his tongue, and she shivered, her breath coming in shallow, erratic pants. "What isn't fair, sweet?" he whispered, rubbing his hand over her waist and down the curve of her hip. His other hand held her anchored against him, and he moved it lower to cup her buttock and languidly knead the rounded softness.

"That you should feel so good," she said breathlessly. Her head was spinning as it never had before. "That you should taste so good." She threaded her fingers through his thick hair.

"I could lodge an identical complaint against you," he said in a raspy voice, then skimmed his tongue along the underside of her lips.

A soft moan escaped her throat. A second later his hard mouth closed over hers. Her lips parted instantly and his tongue penetrated to the moist warmth within, rubbing against her tongue, drawing it into his mouth, then returning to probe every sweet, secret hollow. The kiss grew deeper and deeper, their bodies strained and clung. Both lost all sense of time and place, so completely abandoned were they to the storm of passion that engulfed them.

Neither noticed when the elevator ground to a halt. And then: "Oh!" There was a high-pitched girlish giggle, followed by a hearty masculine chuckle and a low whistle. Case and Sharla sprang apart to see three people standing outside the open elevator doors.

Case stared at the dark-haired, dark-eyed trio.

He immediately recognized the petite nurse standing between the two medical students. Beth
Shakarian. And the two young men? The resemblance was unmistakable. They had to be the two
Shakarian cousins in the Hospital Center's affili-
ated medical school. He stifled a groan.

"Sharla!" Beth and the med students exclaimed
in unison.

Case glanced down at Sharla. The unshakable,
confident physician he'd seen in the Intensive Care
Nursery had been replaced by a vulnerable woman
with passion-swollen lips who was blushing as she
smoothed her hair with trembling fingers. The
sight of her moved him in a way that he could not
quite define. Nor could he accept it. Casey Flynn
believed in keeping things light, casual, and
unmoving.

"Looks like the Armenians have landed," he said
coolly, slipping both arms around Sharla's waist to
hold her in front of him. He was well aware that his
arousal was in extreme evidence.

Sharla felt the burgeoning strength of him
against her. Her pulses pounded in her ears with
the force of a jackhammer. "Hi." She managed a
weak smile at the stunned trio. "Case, as you've
already guessed, these are my cousins—Beth, Alex,
and George Shakarian."

"I didn't know that Dr. Flynn was your boy-
friend, Sharla," Beth said ingenuously.

"He's not." Sharla looked at the floor, acutely
conscious of Case's arms around her, of the inexo-
rable power of his hard masculine frame. And of
the disapproving stares of her two male cousins.
"We—he—was just wishing me a happy birthday."

"May I make a suggestion?" Alex said, his dark
gaze fixed sternly on Case. "From now on, convey
your good wishes in a less public place, Dr. Flynn.
Sharla is well respected around here. We won't
stand for her reputation being compromised in
any way."

"Yeah," George seconded fiercely. "What if some-one else had been the ones to find you two?"

"I was thinking much the same thing," Case said dryly. "Of all the thousands of people who use this elevator daily, what . . . luck that you three hap-pened along." Sharla scowled and tried to move away from him, but he didn't release her. "If you'll excuse us, we'll be on our way," he concluded smoothly.

The cousins rather reluctantly moved aside to let them pass. "Sharla," George called after them. He added something in a totally incomprehensible language that Case had never heard before. Sharla replied in a quietly reassuring voice.

"What was that?" Case asked, following her down the corridor that led to the side exit to the employee parking lot.

"Armenian," she replied. Her cheeks were burn-ing. *Watch your step, Sharla,* her cousin George had said. *It's not unusual for previously sensible women to make complete fools of themselves on turning thirty.* This from her twenty-two-year-old cousin! She used to baby-sit for him! And now he felt the need to warn her against making a sexual fool of herself. She was utterly humiliated.

"You speak *Armenian*?" Case sounded incredulous.

"Of course. We all do. We grew up speaking it." She pushed open the door and stepped outside. The sky was still light and the warm September breeze swirled gently around them. "Unfortu-nately, some of my older cousins' children aren't learning it."

"I can hardly blame their parents for not teach-ing them. A working knowledge of Armenian isn't exactly a requirement for getting along in today's society."

His flippancy irked her. "Says the inestimable Dr. Flynn. A qualified expert in getting along in today's society."

"And now she picks a quarrel to displace her sexual frustration." He grinned rakishly. "I can think of a far more direct—and pleasurable—way to take care of sexual frustration, Sharla."

"Oh, I have no doubts on that score, Dr. Flynn." She glowered at him. "And I'm *not* sexually frustrated. I'm embarrassed and—and disgusted with myself. Maybe being caught necking in an elevator is commonplace to you, but it's not to me."

He laughed. "Maybe a good girl like you needs a bad guy like me to loosen her up a little." He reached out and caught her hand. "Come home with me, Sharla."

Her heart slammed against her rib cage. "No."

"I want you." They were standing under the overhang which sheltered the physicians' section of the parking lot. Case leaned against his white Lotus Esprit Turbo and pulled her to him, encircling her waist with his hands to anchor her securely against him. "And you want me." When she opened her mouth to speak, he placed one long finger over her lips, effectively silencing her. "Don't bother denying it, honey. You went up in flames when I kissed you in the elevator. We're both hot for each other, and we're going to end up in bed together sooner or later so—"

"I should save us the trouble of waiting until later?" she asked wryly.

He lowered his head and rubbed her nose with his, then nibbled lightly on her lips. "Exactly."

Sharla fought the urge to relax against him, to open her mouth under his and lure him inside. He was so big, so strong and warm and hard. And he possessed the power to arouse her as no other man ever had. Her body seemed to respond to him of its own accord while her mind spun off in a sensual whirl.

His big hands caressed her, molding her to him while he kissed her cheeks, her jawline, the graceful curve of her neck. It took great effort on her part not to close her eyes, not to melt into him with a sigh of longing. She wanted him. Too much.

For a crazy moment Sharla considered tossing aside everything she was and everything she believed in for one wild night with him. It would be unlike anything she'd ever known, she was sure of that. Case was able to evoke a reckless passion in her she'd never dreamed she—calm, sensible, industrious Sharla Shakarian—was capable of.

Case felt her resolve wavering. She was on the verge of allowing herself to cede control to him, and he moved quickly to cement his gains. "Come with me, pet," he whispered seductively, catching her earlobe between his teeth at the same moment as his hands slid upward to close possessively over her breasts. "It's going to be so good for us, sweet. So very good."

Sharla closed her eyes dreamily. His voice wrapped about her like warm silk. His lips and hands knew exactly *where* to touch her, *how* to touch her to make her weak and soft and hot. He was so exciting, so experienced, so smooth . . .

Experienced. Smooth. Her thoughts were like a life preserver thrown to a drowning victim. She clutched at them and felt herself begin to surface. He was exciting and experienced and smooth, and he had done these things, said these things to how many countless other women?

She opened her eyes. Sanity had returned with the blunt slam of a sledgehammer. "No, Case."

He tightened his grip and stared down at her, his blue eyes assessing. "Yes, Sharla."

She stiffened and tried to pull away. "It was a good try, Case. I felt as if I were sinking in quicksand for a few minutes there, but I've managed to get out. Now let me go, please."

Instead, he kept one arm firmly around her shoulders and pulled a set of keys from his pocket with his other hand. "This is my car." He nodded at the Lotus. "Get in, honey."

"Case, I don't seem to be getting through to you. I—"

"Oh, you've gotten through to me loud and clear,

honey. Your body has told me all I need to know."
He inserted the key and unlocked the car door.
"Inside, honey."

"Will you *please* stop calling me 'honey'? And
will you listen to what I'm trying to tell you? I'm not
going home with you, Case. Maybe my—my body
wants to, but my mind refuses to go along with it. I
don't indulge in casual sex and I'm not about to
start at the ripe old age of thirty."

"There wouldn't be anything casual about it,
Sharla. The sex between us is going to be damn
explosive and you know it."

She sighed with exasperation. "Then let me put
it another way. I don't indulge in explosive sex with
a man I've only known a few days."

It was Case's turn to sigh. "Sharla, you don't
have to play hard-to-get. You've already got my
attention."

"I'm not playing hard-to-get, Case, I *am* hard to
get. I have to have more than a man's momentary
attention. I don't want sex without trust and love
and mutual respect. That has to come with it to
give it meaning for me."

"For Pete's sake, Sharla, is that what this is all
about? Of course I'll respect you!"

"Mmm-hmm." She had to laugh. "You're getting
desperate, Case. You're falling back on one of the
world's three biggest lies. Let's see now, what are
the other two? 'Your check is in the mail' is one,
and—"

"Sharla, this is nothing to joke about!"

"It's no use, Case." She reached up and laid her
fingertips lightly against his cheek. "I'm not going
to bed with you. So why don't you get out your little
black book—I'm sure you have one the size of the
DC phone directory—and call up a lady who's willing? You won't have any trouble finding one, I'm
sure."

"Okay." He straightened, his voice, his expression cool. "That's exactly what I'll do. And you're
right, I won't have any trouble finding one."

Sharla gave a quick little nod of her head, feeling ridiculously sad. For him, for herself. Just the prebirthday blues, she assured herself. One should expect a few such moments upon turning thirty. "Good night, Case." She turned to walk briskly to her car, a sporty little silver-gray Honda CRX.

Case watched her go. She was absolutely right to leave, he told himself. She wanted sex with commitment and he wasn't the man to give it to her. He wanted freewheeling, good-time sex, with no promises, no meaning, and no strings. And he could call anyone in a bookful of names to get it.

He watched her climb into her small bubble-shaped car. The sports car fanatic in him admired the lines of it. He'd heard good things about that car. A columnist in *Car and Driver* magazine had rated the small front-wheel drive CRX as the zippiest, nimblest two-passenger car on the road, the consummate vehicle for urban traffic driving. Case climbed into his Lotus. Yes, he'd love to take Sharla's zippy little car for a spin on the Capitol Beltway.

Sharla had been driving for a while when she began to wonder whether Case was following her. Of course, he'd had to follow her out of the parking lot. There was only one exit. And she'd considered it mere coincidence when he'd made a left turn onto Michigan Avenue NW, just as she had. But when he continued to tail her through the fourth— the fifth!—traffic light, she began to wonder. Was he following her? Or did he live in one of the apartment complexes near hers?

But when she pulled her little car into a space in front of her apartment building, and he pulled the Lotus into the space next to hers, her stomach did a double flip. Case Flynn did *not* live in the Spring Garden Apartments.

She was reaching for the door handle when he

opened her door and offered her his hand. She took it, allowing him to help her from her car.

"You followed me," she said, staring up at him, her hand still in his. His blue eyes were unfathomable, his face an unreadable mask.

"Of course I can keep a secret," he said.

"What?" She was utterly baffled by the non sequitur.

"That's the third biggest lie. 'I'll respect you in the morning,' 'the check is in the mail,' and 'of course I can keep a secret.' The world's three biggest lies."

She grinned. "What about the infamous, 'We'll have your car ready by noon'?"

He considered it. "It's a contender, but not big enough to be one of the Big Three."

"I guess you're right. Thanks for setting me straight, Dr. Flynn." Still smiling, she removed her hand from his and took a step toward the building's front door. "Good night, Case."

He stepped in front of her, blocking her way. "I like your car."

"Thank you."

"I've never driven a CRX."

"This is the Si model. It's great fun to drive."

"You . . . uh, know about cars?"

"With two brothers and thirteen male first cousins, how could I *not* know about cars?" She tilted her head and looked up at him, laughter in her black eyes. "I'll let you drive it sometime."

"How about right now?"

She smiled sweetly. "You'd like to borrow my car to pick up your date tonight?"

His hands closed over her shoulders. "I was thinking more along the lines of driving you and me to the nearest Mexican restaurant. Didn't we pass one a few blocks down the road?"

She nodded. "The Alamo. They call their food Tex-Mex."

"Chili so hot it'll make your eyes water?" he asked hopefully. "Let's go."

She stepped away from him. "I don't think it would be a very good idea, Case."

"I'm sure they serve a mild version of the chili too."

"Oh, it's not the chili I'm objecting to. The hotter the better for me." She met his eyes, her expression suddenly serious. "Case, I haven't changed my mind about one-night stands. And I don't feel like going through the whole argument with you again after dinner. Call someone else."

He felt himself being drawn into the ebony depths of her eyes. Call someone else, she'd said. The truth of the matter was, he didn't want to call anyone else. The unwelcome realization had struck him back in the hospital parking lot when he'd watched her climb into her car and drive away from him.

"I don't want to call anyone else," he admitted grudgingly. He wanted to be with Sharla, only Sharla. No one else would do. It was the first time he had admitted it to himself. It was the first time he'd felt this way. He'd always viewed his sexual partners as virtually interchangeable. If one wasn't available, he would cheerfully call the next name on the list.

He looked down at Sharla, his gaze lingering on her mouth before trailing over her neat, slender figure. It was unbelievable, it was disconcerting, it was downright terrifying, but there wasn't a woman in his thick little black book who could serve as a replacement for Sharla tonight.

She watched him intently as he studied her. "You'd rather have dinner and a sexless evening with me than go to bed with another woman?"

"That's right, rub it in," he grumbled, then exhaled sharply. "Dammit, it's true."

He looked aghast at the notion. Sharla studied his disgruntled expression and fought back a smile.

Case saw her lips quivering and flashed a fierce

scowl. "I'm glad you find it so hilarious, lady. Go ahead, laugh!"

"You look like you're about to be forced to take a dose of paraldehyde." She named the nastiest smelling and tasting medicine she could think of. Case was glowering at her, challenging her to laugh at him. She had never been one to resist a challenge. She laughed.

"You've put some kind of Armenian curse on me," he accused her. Much against his will, he felt himself starting to smile. She was irrepressible. And so damned appealing. And she possessed the ability to reach him on a level no other woman had ever touched. She made him smile when he ought to be irritated, and she made him want her company *out* of bed.

"Ah, yes," she said, "The old Armenian curse I learned at my grandmother's knee. You should run—not walk—away from me, Casey Flynn."

"You're right, I should." Instead, he impulsively picked her up and sat her on the sloping hood of her car, positioning himself between her knees. He curved his hands over her hips and pulled her tightly into the masculine cradle of his thighs.

"Case," she protested breathlessly. She glanced down, and the sight of her thighs hugging his waist caused a deliciously sharp ache deep within her. Thankfully, her black skirt was pleated and had enough material to prevent it from hiking up too far. Which wasn't to say it hadn't done some hiking. Her long, slim legs were exposed to mid-thigh.

Case smoothed his hands over the nylon-clad length of her thighs, then wrapped his arms around her waist, bringing her against the hard strength of his chest. Her breasts strained against the solid muscular wall. There was nowhere else for her to put her arms but around his neck, and she did, burying her face in the hollow of his shoulder. "This is crazy, Case," she whispered.

His lips tasted the warm, scented spot at the

base of her throat, then moved upward along the milk-white curve of her neck. "I know." He rubbed her back with his palms, his strokes long and languorous. "Tell me to get the hell out of your life, Sharla."

"I should." She snuggled closer. "I really should. We're so different, *too* different."

"We're worlds apart." His arms tightened possessively. "We have absolutely nothing in common."

"Nothing but medicine and a preference for sports cars and hot chili." She pressed her mouth against the hard, tanned column of his neck. Her nipples were taut and straining and aching to be touched. Instinctively, she rubbed them against his chest, seeking the sensuous pressure to soothe the ache. He was hard and thick between her legs, and her body arched against him, aching, empty, desperately striving to fill the void.

She let her feelings take over. She'd never fully known the sensation of giving in, of letting someone take control of her while her mind spun wildly away, releasing her from all thoughts, all worries. The only demands Case would make were physical ones, and she was hungry to meet them.

And then suddenly, abruptly, she was on her feet, standing alone beside the car. Case had lifted her down from the hood and put her away from him. He stood with his back to her, his hands jammed into his pockets.

Sharla leaned back against the car, her legs wobbly and weak, her breathing painfully erratic. She tried to swallow, tried to speak, but those functions seemed to be temporarily out of order.

"I can't play these games, Sharla." His voice was as unsteady as she knew hers would be, had she been able to find it. "I won't!"

"I—I don't blame you." She found her voice and it was even unsteadier than Case's. "It's much too tough on the constitution. I prefer to keep a normal hormone balance myself."

He muttered an expletive, and his shoulders

began to shake strangely. She stared at him curiously. "Dammit, Sharla!" Abruptly, he turned to face her. To her utter disbelief, he was laughing.

"I'm strung out, my body aches all the way up to my teeth, and you make one of your stupid, matter-of-fact comments that fractures me."

She smiled slowly. "Would you rather I wept or raged at you?"

"Yes! I can handle weepy, raging women. I simply tune them out and ignore them."

"And put a black mark beside their name in your little book?" she guessed. "Three strikes against them and they're out?"

"One strike. I don't have time to waste on weepers or ragers."

"The competition among them must be awesome," she said. "I guess it's a good thing I never made your book. I'd have been inked out already."

"You would've been—for not showing the proper respect for my very accomplished line." He wanted to touch her soft, flushed cheek, but didn't permit himself to do so. He didn't trust himself to merely touch her and withdraw. And he had to withdraw. It was imperative to maintain his distance from her. *She* was getting to *him*, and that was not in his game plan.

They stared at each other for a long, silent moment. She was wildly attracted to him, Sharla admitted to herself. And she liked him too. He was a cheerfully unabashed, self-admitted rogue, and it was stimulating to match wits with him. But she instinctively sensed that there could be something more than light banter and sex between them. Something deep and rich and lasting. It was as if the easygoing rogue were daring her to peel away the layers of his carefully constructed facade and reveal the man trapped within.

Was that inner man capable of loving her as she wanted to be loved, as she *needed* to be loved? Sharla didn't know. But he was worth taking a chance on, she was sure of that. She had never been one to shy away from the risk of emotional involvement. To her anything—anyone—worth having was worth the risk of pain.

She stared deeply into Case's eyes. She knew he didn't feel that way. He felt that nothing—no one—was worth the risk of pain. He'd made a point of avoiding emotional commitments and involvements. And he would walk away from her right now rather than take an emotional risk to discover something wonderful.

If she wanted any kind of relationship with Casey Flynn—and she did, she acknowledged achingly—she was going to have to be the one who took the risks and the chances.

"Since I'm out of your black book before I ever made it in," she said, "shall I assume that your invitation to have dinner at The Alamo is null and void?" Her voice was light, but her gaze never wavered.

"Shall *I* assume that you'll only have dinner with me if I don't try to take you to bed afterward?"

"Afraid so."

"Well." He appeared to be considering it. "I *would* like to drive your car. And I'm starving and a big bowl of Texas chili sounds mighty tempting." He didn't add that the prospect of spending more time in her company was the biggest lure of all. He wasn't about to admit that to her! Case Flynn had an entire repertoire of romantic lines and phrases, but he only used them when he didn't mean them. "I guess I'll have dinner with you tonight, Sharla, since it is your birthday tomorrow and all."

"How magnificent of you! And if I ask really nicely, I bet you'll even let me pay the check!" She handed him her car keys.

She was grinning, he thought, not at all offended by his flippancy or his thoroughly unromantic invitation to dinner. Sharla could hold her own with him, he realized with grudging admiration. He couldn't crush her with a thoughtless word or an angry look. This wasn't a woman who would lose her identity in him, who would drain him by making him her sole reason for existence.

Where had all these insights come from? he asked himself mockingly. He'd never been one to analyze a person or situation that wasn't related to the field of medicine. Now that he was forty, was he going to turn into an introspective Phil Donahue type? What a thought!

Once inside the car, Sharla flicked on the radio and music filled the silver-gray interior. Case pulled the CRX out onto the road. "This *is* a snappy little car." He was quite pleased with it. "Handles beautifully."

"I thought about getting a Mustang GT or a Corvette," Sharla said. "But a friend talked me into this and I'm glad he did."

They discussed the merits, performances, and prices of various sports cars during the short drive to the restaurant. Sharla wasn't as well versed as Case, but she knew enough to keep up her end of the conversation.

"Who's the friend who talked you into getting the CRX?" he asked casually as he opened the car door for Sharla and assisted her out.

"It was Jason Fletcher."

"Fletcher? The cretin down on ortho?" Actually, Jason Fletcher, a skilled orthopedic surgeon, was a respected colleague and a friendly rival of Case's for many of the nurses' hearts. This was the first time that Case had ever thought of his old pal as a cretin. "Fletch the Lech?" Case frowned. "Do you have something going with him?"

"With Jason?" Sharla laughed. "No way. But he can be a lot of fun. We're very good friends."

"Are you?" Case didn't like the idea. Not at all. And he hated the idea that he was feeling . . . *jealous*?

"When I first met Jason, we had a conversation quite similar to the one you and I had. He wanted me to go to bed with him and I said I didn't go in for casual affairs. He said he didn't go in for any other kind. So we decided to be friends—and we are."

Case took her arm and guided her to an empty booth. "So we're fated to be friends? Is that what you're trying to tell me?" *Sorry, honey. If there were ever two people destined to go to bed together, it's you and me.*

Sharla read the unspoken message in his eyes, and answered with one of her own. *If and when we go to bed together, it's going to be different from any affair you've ever had, Casey Flynn.*

Case swallowed. "So . . ." He was suddenly extremely interested in the menu. "What are you having besides chili?"

Three

"Sharla, Jack Knowlton is admitting a patient to maternity this afternoon," Mel Chehovitz told Sharla the moment she entered his small office on the hospital's pediatric floor. She'd found a note summoning her there when she'd arrived at the Intensive Care Nursery earlier that morning. Jack Knowlton was a highly respected perinatologist, an obstetrician who specialized in caring for women in high-risk pregnancies. Sharla had often treated the babies born to Jack's patients. They were usually preemies, multiple births, or infants with complications due to their mothers' medical problems.

"What's the mother's problem?" she asked, her interest immediately piqued.

"She's thirty-one years old and five and a half months pregnant." Mel lit his pipe. "And her last sonogram showed eight fetuses."

"Eight?" Sharla gasped. "*Eight?*" Her voice rose on a squeak of incredulity.

Mel nodded. "She was taking fertility drugs, of course. Jack had her dosage carefully monitored, but she seems to be one of the few who produces multiple eggs while on the drug. She gave birth to quadruplets five years ago and lost all of them."

"How terrible for her," Sharla said softly. She'd seen it happen over and over. Babies born in multiple births were doubly at risk due to their lower birth weights and high incidence of prematurity. Multiples came fast and early. Often only one or, tragically, none survived. She'd wept in frustration more than once after such cases. "Oh, Mel, eight! She won't be able to carry that many much longer, and they'll be so small!"

"Jack thinks he can hold off labor till she's seven and a half, maybe eight months along, Sharla. That would give at least some of them a fighting chance."

Sharla didn't hold out much hope for prolonging the pregnancy that long. A woman's body simply couldn't accommodate so many babies past a certain point. She didn't voice her doubts, for Mel was a great one for thinking positively. Normally she was, too, but in this case . . . Eight babies! "What is the term for eight born at the same time, Mel?"

"Octuplets. There've actually been recorded births of octuplets in China and Mexico. None have survived, but some of *these* children are going to make it, Sharla. I'm assigning you as their primary physician. I can't think of another neonatologist anywhere who'll do a better job."

His display of faith overwhelmed her. "Mel, you know I'll do everything I can. But *eight* . . .!"

"The Hospital Center isn't going to release any news until the birth is impending, then I suppose we can expect a media circus. As the infants' doctor, you'll have to meet with reporters and the like. I'm sure you can handle the press without any problems."

She thought of the hoopla that had surrounded other newsworthy multiple births across the nation. Circus was an apt description. She took a deep breath. "I'd like to talk to the mother. I want to have her approve me as her babies' doctor."

"Of course. She's to be admitted shortly after noon. Call on her at your own convenience." Mel stood up, and Sharla did too. "And, Sharla, happy birthday. You've achieved a career milestone on a milestone birthday, eh?"

Sharla was a little dazed. Being primary physician for a set of octuplets was a career milestone, all right. She thought of the mother, who'd already lost four children and now faced the very real possibility of losing eight more. "No!" She spoke aloud, her voice full of determination and fire. "Mel, we're *not* going to lose them all."

Mel beamed his approval. "That's the old Armenian fighting spirit!"

The nursery staff bid a fond good-bye to Baby Douglas Pearson, who was dressed in a blue hand-knit outfit, wrapped in a matching blanket, and placed firmly into the arms of his proud father. The mother embraced each of the nurses, and there were tears in everyone's eyes. For Sharla, watching the happy parents carry home a healthy baby whose very survival had once been in question was one of the most rewarding aspects of her profession. Mrs. Pearson gave her a fierce hug.

"Send us a picture of Douglas for our rogues' gallery," Sharla said. She indicated the large bulletin board on which snapshots of former patients, now chubby toddlers or sturdy children, were proudly displayed. Both Pearsons promised that they would.

What would it be like to bring your own baby home to the room carefully and lovingly decorated just for him, or her? Sharla asked herself. She had wondered that more than once. And now, on her thirtieth birthday, it seemed only natural to wonder a little more wistfully. Her biological time clock was ticking away, and she'd always wanted a child. She gazed at the tiny infants sleeping amidst the tangle of tubes, wires, and machines in the nursery and her thoughts turned immediately from herself to the unborn octuplets whose birth would cause a worldwide sensation. Would it be possible to make medical history and save them all? The prospect excited her. If only they could . . .

"Going to lunch?" Brian Cranston asked her, and Sharla snapped from her reverie.

She glanced at the wall clock and nodded. "Since it's my birthday, I think I'll forgo the nutritious fare in the cafeteria and splurge on junk food in the snack bar."

"Sounds good to me," Brian said. "Let's go."

They turned the corner to the elevators at the same moment that Case Flynn rounded the same corner to the nursery. "Case!" Sharla exclaimed, her face lighting at the sight of him.

Case came to an immediate halt. "Oh . . . uh . . . Hi, Sharla." It was easy for him to appear nonchalant. Only he knew that he was far from feeling that way. The sight of Sharla had sent a charge of high-voltage pleasure through him.

Brian glanced from Sharla to Case. "I think I'll head on down to lunch," he said, and quickly absented himself.

Case and Sharla faced each other in the bustling corridor. "I was just on my way to lunch," she said. "Care to join me?" Her heart did a crazy little leap. Had Case been coming to see her? It seemed likely. Didn't it?

When he had walked her to her apartment door after their dinner last night, she hadn't been sure when—or if—she would see him again. Not that they hadn't had a marvelous time at The Alamo. They had. They'd laughed at each other as they broke into a sweat and gulped water after a few mouthfuls of the throat-burning chili. They'd discovered that each of them had vacationed in Mexico, and compared notes on their respective trips. They'd also swapped med-school tales and residency tales and Hospital Center tales, the humorous stories and the horror stories. It had been past ten-thirty when Case had delivered her safely to her door and left without even trying to kiss her good night. The end or the beginning? Sharla had lain awake for quite a while wondering.

And now he was here, gazing at her with those blue eyes, his expression faintly mocking. "Lunch, hmm?" he said. "I guess I have time to grab a quick bite. As long as it's not the cafeteria. I prefer food from vending machines to the institutional slop the cafeteria dishes out."

"You mean you don't like Halibut Surprise and Meat Loaf Croquettes?" she teased, naming two of the least popular dishes served there.

"In the immortal word of my two-year-old nephew—'yuck!' "

She laughed. "I guess it's the snack bar for us, then." It seemed perfectly natural for Case to grip her elbow and guide her toward the elevators. Both cars were jammed with the lunchtime crowd; there was no chance of a secluded tryst this time. Sharla cast a furtive glance at Case and found him watching her. Was he thinking the same thing? she wondered. Remembering the heated passion that had flared between them in this very elevator?

He met her gaze and arched his dark brows suggestively. She felt a flush suffuse her cheeks and tilted her chin primly. His soft laughter echoed through her head. "I'm remembering, Sharla," he said in a voice so low only she could hear. "Every part of me is remembering."

"You're a devil, Case Flynn," she admonished severely, and he grinned unrepentantly.

"And you're a witch, Sharla. I guess that makes us evenly matched."

Case pronounced the cheeseburgers and french fries served by the snack bar as "not up to fast-food quality, but superior to anything served in the hospital cafeteria." He and Sharla sat at a small table for two in the crowded snack bar.

Sharla watched with amusement as nurses of various ages attempted to catch Case's eye. A few came over to the table to say hello to him. He politely introduced Sharla to each one.

"This must be like dining with Paul Newman," she remarked after the fifth such interruption. "You certainly have a slew of devoted fans, Case."

Normally, Case would have enjoyed the attention. He might even have relished this evidence of his attraction for the opposite sex. But today he found it embarrassing, even annoying. Sharla's amusement smacked of condescension. She certainly wasn't jealous, and he was foolishly annoyed that she wasn't.

"Let's get out of here," he muttered the moment she'd finished her cheeseburger. He pulled her forcefully away from the crowded snack bar, oblivious to the stares of the interested onlookers. Sharla kept pace with his determined stride. She really had no choice, as his big hand was fastened firmly around her wrist.

He didn't speak until they were in the tower building that housed the Shock/Trauma Unit. "Do you have time to come to the staff lounge with me?" he asked briskly.

She glanced at her watch. "I have a meeting with a group of pediatric interns in twenty minutes, but I'm free until then."

"Good." He led her into a spacious lounge on the floor above the ST's admitting area. There were several comfortable armchairs, a couch, some tables, a few pots of coffee, and several vending machines scattered throughout the room. A nurse was munching on a sandwich while reading a newspaper. Two doctors were absorbed in an intense discussion of whether the soda machine should stock New Coke or Coca-Cola Classic.

Case led Sharla to a far corner of the lounge and pulled something from the deep pocket of his white trousers. It was a small gift-wrapped package. "Happy birthday," he said, and thrust the package at her, feeling uncomfortable and ill at ease. Spontaneous gift-giving did not come naturally to him.

He'd surprised himself when he'd stopped at the hospital gift shop earlier that morning.

"Oh, Case, how sweet of you!" Sharla's eyes were glowing, her face radiant. She ripped off the wrapping paper with the zealous enthusiasm of a child at a birthday party. "I love it!" she exclaimed, holding up the miniature metal model of a Honda CRX. "And it's gray, just like my car!"

Case watched her, pleased with her delight in the gift, yet embarrassed with the gift itself. Wasn't it foolishly trivial for a woman's thirtieth birthday? For the first time in years, he felt vulnerable and unsure of himself. A most unnerving experience for the legendary cool and confident Casey Flynn. "I . . . uh, should have sent you roses. Or bought you a box of candy."

"No, this is perfect!" Impulsively, she flung her arms around his neck. Case probably sent flowers and candy by rote, she thought. They could be exceedingly impersonal tokens. This little gift was special, just for her, and it had a meaning for both of them. Perhaps he'd just realized that himself. She grinned against his starched white coat. "It was so thoughtful of you, Case."

His arms came around to enfold her. He was not sweet or thoughtful, he knew that. He'd had enough irate lovers call him unemotional, thoughtless, and indifferent, and he'd always agreed. Nor was he one for impulsively picking up whimsical little gifts. Yet he'd done just that today, for Sharla. His arms tightened around her as he inhaled the scent of her. She smelled fresh and clean, a light fragrance of floral cologne and baby powder and—

"Ah, the intoxicating aroma of hexachlorophene." He leaned back, his eyes gleaming with humor. "The ultimate medical turn-on."

She wriggled loose and pretended to be insulted, but her bright-eyed grin gave her away. Case resisted the urge to pull her back to him. "I guess you have plans for tonight," he said casually, and inwardly groaned at his lack of finesse. The last time he'd used that approach was when he'd said to a girl, "I guess you wouldn't want to go to the movies with me, huh?" He'd been all of thirteen.

"My cousin Clare and her husband are having all the cousins over for a birthday dinner at her house." Sharla noticed that he was carefully looking away from her. "Would you like to come? Clare's planning a buffet and she always has plenty of food."

"Armenian dishes?"

Sharla smiled. "A few of our favorites. But mostly good old American things like fried chicken and ham and potato salad."

"Well . . ." Case considered it. He had assiduously avoided meeting family members of anyone he'd ever dated. He'd never wanted to encourage any false hopes of a serious involvement. "I'd better not, Sharla."

"Hmm, you may be right. After all, Alex and Georgie are liable to truss you up and hold you captive while Father Kasabian—he's our priest at St. Gregory's Armenian Church—pronounces us man and wife."

Case reddened slightly. Put like that, it *did* sound absurd. Still, he had the reticence of a lifetime to contend with, and meeting a woman's family seemed to scream of emotional entanglement, of serious involvement, of—he swallowed—marriage. His face hardened. "Sorry, Sharla."

She shrugged. "It's okay, Case." What else could she say? His thoughts had visibly played across his face, and she'd read them loud and clear. He thought that meeting her family would be too serious a step for the man who'd vowed never to become serious about any relationship with any woman. This was, after all, the same Case Flynn who would rather be dead than married. Which brought her to a point she'd been curious about. "Case, you've mentioned two nephews, a two-year-old and a one-month-old. I take it they're not the children of your sister who prefers tombstones to wedding rings?"

Case laughed. Her phraseology amused him. And he was inordinately relieved that she wasn't going to fuss about his refusing to come to her birthday party. "You take it right. I have two sisters. My little sister, Shay, is the one who's married and has the two boys, Scotty and Brandon. Candy is my twin sister and she shares my . . . uh, philosophy of life."

"I see. Is Candy a doctor too?"

"Candy? Oh, no! Candy doesn't like to repair and rebuild, as we so often do in medicine. She takes great pleasure in destroying." Something about the way he said it, the blue ice in his eyes, chilled Sharla. "Candy is a renowned divorce lawyer. A bomber, or barracuda, as they're respectfully called in the profession. She tears apart what no man is supposed to put asunder." He laughed a cynical laugh, one that Sharla didn't like hearing. At this particular moment she didn't like him very much. Or his twin sister.

"I'd better go," she said. "It's almost time for my meeting." She was unaware of how her voice had cooled.

But Case noticed. He also noticed that the warmth had disappeared from her eyes. They were as cold as onyx gemstones. Though he'd deliberately chosen to antagonize her, he now, perversely, wanted her warmth and her smiles. "Sharla, I—"

"Good-bye, Case. Thank you very much for my present." She walked away from him and didn't look back. If she had, she would have seen him staring after her, his face bleak, his blue eyes brooding.

"But she seems better, Dr. Flynn?" the young woman pleaded, her eyes swimming with tears. "She survived the surgery and her blood pressure is more stable than it was last night, so she *must* be better!"

"She's holding her own, Janet," Case said kindly, patting the woman's arm. "It's a good sign. We can't expect any better than that at this point."

"It's a good sign," repeated a weary-eyed young man. "She's going to make it, isn't she, Dr. Flynn?"

"Your mother's a fighter, Tom, and she's in excellent physical condition. All those are pluses she has going for her." Case had been through similar scenes countless times during his career as a trauma surgeon. The distraught family clung to any shred of hope, however small. They literally begged him for reassurance, and unless it would be cruelly wrong to delude them, Case tried to provide the positive feedback these panicked families so desperately needed.

He was worried about his current patient, Mary Margaret Aiello, a sixty-five-year-old widowed grandmother who'd been admitted to the ST Unit last night after her car had been sideswiped by a pickup truck. She'd suffered multiple internal injuries and had been in surgery for eight and a half hours. Case had been the performing surgeon. He'd first met the woman's family, two sons and two daughters, all married and accompanied by their spouses, after the extensive operation.

He liked the family. They were well spoken and, most of all, considerate and supportive of each other. Some families weren't. He'd witnessed a score of ugly scenes in which family members used the sudden tragedy to go after one another tooth and claw. Mary Margaret Aiello's family was clearly concerned for her and for each other as well. Case was impressed by their solidarity and strength.

He talked to the family a while longer, offering them as much hope and support as he could. Mrs. Aiello's age made her somewhat unique in the Shock/Trauma Unit. Most of the patients admitted there were younger, ranging from their teens to their forties. Accidents seemed to be a particular hazard to younger people. And, tragically, patients of Mrs. Aiello's age often didn't survive the trip to the community hospital, let alone the transfer to the Hospital Center.

But, as Case had told her children, Mary Margaret was a physically strong woman and exceptionally fit for her age. One of the daughters had told him Mary Margaret taught tennis and swimming to children at their community center. She walked two miles a day and was an avid bicyclist and a nonsmoker. She had a lot in her favor. If any sixty-five-year-old woman could survive a serious accident, Mary Margaret Aiello could. And Case desperately wanted her to. The more he learned about his patient, the more he observed and got to know the family, the more he was determined to save her. This was a grandmother, a mother, a woman who was loved and needed.

"She's going to pull through this," he said with absolute conviction. The Aiello sons and daughters clung to each other, their faces reflecting both hope and agony. "Your mother's going to make it."

When Dr. Flynn spoke those words with his quiet authority, the families responded as if they'd been talking directly to God. "Oh, thank you, Dr. Flynn!" Mary Jo, the younger daughter, gave him a quick, emotional hug. Case patted her shoulder. No, he wasn't going to let the Aiellos' mother die.

The Aiellos were very much on his mind as he strode to the cafeteria to buy fifteen cups of coffee for the staff. The unit's coffeepot was currently out of service, which qualified as something of a disaster for the coffee-addicted staff. Everyone had taken a turn making a coffee run to the cafeteria, and this time it was Case's turn. He didn't mind; he needed a brief spell away from the unit. He'd been there for the past thirteen hours straight.

Was it fate that the first person he spotted in the cafeteria was Sharla Shakarian? He stifled a groan. He hadn't seen Sharla since her birthday last week. There had been more than a few times when he'd been tempted to steal up to the Intensive Care Nursery for a glimpse of her, but he'd restrained himself. There was no point in seeing her, he'd argued with himself. She was family-oriented, committed to commitment. She was the type of woman a devil-may-care bachelor like himself should avoid like the proverbial plague.

Sharla didn't see him, and he intended to enter the food line without speaking to her. He watched her, his eyes drinking in every detail. She was sitting alone, her head slightly bowed. She was contemplating her coffee cup with the intense concentration of a first-year medical student studying *Gray's Anatomy*. Her face was devoid of its usual animation. Case frowned. She looked depressed.

Before he knew what he was doing, he'd left the food line and was striding over to her table. "You look like you've lost your last friend," he said lightly.

She glanced up at him. "No, just Baby Andrews." Her big, dark eyes were sad. "He weighed seven hundred and fifty grams and was born ten weeks early. He was transferred in this morning from Suburban Hospital." She stared sightlessly into her half-empty cup. "And we lost him."

Case pulled up a chair and slipped into it. "Not through any mistake or negligence on your part," he said. He knew instinctively that Sharla practiced impeccable medicine. She was a perfectionist, driven and caring about her patients. Like him.

She sighed. "No, it was nothing we did or didn't do. He was just too small and too weak, poor baby. But what's so frustrating . . ." She made a fist and stared up into Case's eyes. He drew in his breath sharply. She was stunning, vibrant and vital and so alive. He felt the exhaustion of the past hours melt away and a surge of adrenaline flow through him. She had that effect upon him.

"We've saved babies that small, even smaller, Little Bit, for one. But this baby—" Sharla swallowed hard. "Dammit, Case, I don't know what went wrong. We did everything we've done before, but . . . this time . . ." Her voice trailed off.

"Sometimes the patient's constitution just isn't strong enough, Sharla. Sometimes it's a pure fluke. The x factor. Believe me, I've experienced the same thing. A patient who's injured critically will pull through, while the one who should've made it . . ." He sighed. "Doesn't. Those are the cases that drive me nuts."

"The ones that make you toss and turn at night," she said, and he nodded empathetically.

They sat in silence for a few moments. "I have a patient now," Case said at last, "one who's going to make it despite all the stats against her." He briefly outlined Mary Margaret Aiello's accident, surgery, and family. "She's going to pull through," he added, as if daring Sharla to challenge his assertion.

She didn't. She'd immediately identified with the Aiello sons and daughters. "It must be terrible to face the possibility of losing your mother that way."

Case stared at his hands. "My mother was killed in an accident," he blurted out suddenly. "In a bus accident while on her way to work thirteen years ago."

Sharla stared at him. Case was not one to offer much personal information about himself. She sensed that his mother's accident was a subject he seldom discussed. "Then you know exactly what the Aiellos are going through," she said softly. "Has it opened some wounds, Case?"

He shrugged. "I suppose it's set me to wondering what it's like to love a mother, to grieve for one. I wouldn't know. Candy and I shed no tears when our mother died."

His words shocked her. She thought of her own mother, whom she loved dearly. But then, not all mothers were warm and kind and loving like hers.

She was certainly aware of that. She gazed at Case. An unloving mother in a miserable marriage. A sister who made her living sowing bitterness and revenge in divorce cases. A man who avoided emotional involvement and commitment. The pieces clicked into place.

He was watching her, waiting, she knew, to scorn whatever platitudes she might offer. She could almost see him withdrawing, regretting his impulsive confession. "What about your younger sister?" she asked. "Did she feel the same way?"

"Shay? She was only seventeen when our mother was killed, just a kid in high school."

She could tell she'd disarmed him completely by asking about his sister, not himself. Sharla had learned long ago that one might talk more freely about a family member than about oneself and still reveal a lot of personal feelings.

"Shay took our mother's death hard," Case said slowly. "She and Mother genuinely loved each other, you see. I've often thought that that's the reason Shay is capable of sustaining a long-term relationship. And why she's able to love her children. She grew up loved—by a mother and Candy and me."

"You've sustained a long-term relationship with both your sisters," Sharla reminded him. "That's more than some people have managed. You're not a total isolate."

"That's different."

"Is it?"

"Sharla, loving a sister is a lot different from loving in a marriage."

"Maybe so, but it's a start. It proves you're not incapable of love."

He smiled slightly. "You're not going to let me win this one, are you?"

She was ready with another question. "Why didn't your mother love you and your twin sister?"

She hadn't tried to soothe him with empty reassurances of his mother's love, he thought. He respected her for that. And her question diverted him. It was one no one had ever asked. "Kathleen— our mother—was only sixteen when Candy and I were born. Needless to say, she was pregnant when *her* father forced her to marry *our* father, who was and is an irresponsible, egocentric phony four years her senior. You can imagine what a rotten marriage it was—and all it needed was a set of colicky twins."

Sharla could imagine. She nodded her comprehension.

"All I can remember of my childhood is screaming and fighting, drinking and hitting, things being thrown, one or the other parent walking out. And coming back. They were stuck together in one of the world's sickest relationships. And Candy and I were trapped in it too." Case stared into space, remembering. "To his credit, our father was indifferent to us. He never did a damn thing for us, but at least he never beat us or cursed us. We had our mother for that."

"Oh, Case." Impulsively, Sharla covered his hand with her own. Abuse of children struck a deep chord within her.

He smiled tightly. "Our mother didn't dislike me quite as much as she did Candy, whom she simply seemed to hate. Maybe because Candy resembled our father, maybe because she was a difficult baby who became a defiant child."

"Yet she loved your little sister?"

"Shay was born when Candy and I were ten, after my parents' twelfth separation and reconciliation. And whether it was because my mother was older and had gained some maturity or because Shay was a sweet-natured, quiet baby—who knows?— our mother loved her. I was always on the alert for it, but she never mistreated Shay in any way. When Candy and I left home the day after our high-school graduation, I knew we didn't have to worry about leaving Shay with Mother. Thank God for that."

"What became of Shay after your mother's death?"

"Our father was out of the picture, so Candy and I brought her here to DC to live with us." Case smiled at the memory. "Candy and I'd had our own places for years and it was a fiasco when we tried to move back in together. Tell people who say they're staying together for the sake of the kids to forget it, it's a faulty premise. Candy and I fought like cats and dogs, and I finally moved back to my own apartment. Shay came and went between us and it worked out just fine. I'm a loner," he added. "I'm just not capable of living with anyone else."

"You came from a terrible home, yet you managed to put yourself through college and medical school, to become a skilled surgeon who cares for his patients. You gave your younger sister a home when she didn't have one . . ." Sharla gazed at him, her eyes glowing. "You're a man of remarkable strengths and inner resources, Case. I think you're capable of doing anything you set your mind to."

A man of remarkable strengths and inner resources? he repeated to himself. He felt simultaneously warmed and embarrassed by her effusive praise. And the way she'd said it, with her beautiful ebony eyes shining with admiration. He wanted to hear more; he wanted to tell her more. She seemed to understand . . . He could talk, *really talk*, to her.

Sharla knew Case was going to pull back any minute. As he'd shared his painful memories, the two of them had been close and emotionally attuned, and in just a moment he was going to feel threatened and run like hell.

"Hey," he said, "I've been widely lauded for my technical skills as a surgeon and a lover, but never for my inner strengths and resources." He flashed a practiced, devilish grin, mocking the words that meant so much to him. He couldn't seem to handle them any other way.

He was trying to push her away, she thought. She wondered how she knew him so well, but could come up with no answers. She simply understood him, maybe better than he understood himself. "I meant it, Case," she said quietly.

He stood up abruptly. He had to get away from her! If he didn't . . . He was uncharacteristically nervous. He wanted to stay with her too much! "I'm sorry I bored you with my life story." His tone was suddenly cynical and his eyes ice blue, like they'd been when he'd withdrawn from her on her birthday.

But this time Sharla didn't turn cool. Her gaze remained fixed on him, warm and accepting. "You didn't bore me, Case."

He stared down at her silky black hair and wanted to reach out and stroke it so badly, he had to jam his hands into his pockets to prevent himself from doing so. "I've got to go, Sharla. I'm getting coffee for everyone—our pot's broken upstairs—and we caffeine addicts need our fix."

Yes, he was running from her all right. Didn't he realize how much he'd given away? Had he stayed and bantered glibly, she would've known she meant nothing to him.

"So . . . take care, Sharla."

"I will. Good-bye, Case."

"Sharla." He turned around. "How was your birthday party—at your cousin's house?"

She smiled. "It was great. Grandpa and Grandma sent a videotape of the family back in Racine, and we played it on Clare and John's VCR."

"Your grandparents made a videotape?"

"The whole family chipped in and bought them a VCR and portable video camera for their sixtieth wedding anniversary. Now Grandpa is forever making videotapes. He stages them quite creatively. We call him the Armenian Steven Spielberg."

Case laughed. So did Sharla. Their eyes met and something passed between them, something intangible, indescribable, yet very real. Whatever was between them was too powerful for either of them to ignore—or run away from—though Sharla was fairly certain that Case would try to do both. But he would be back, she was *completely* certain of that. Case was as attracted to her as she was to him.

"Say, uh, Sharla . . ." He couldn't seem to drag himself away from her table. "Are there . . . uh, any good Armenian restaurants in the area?"

"Sadly, no. I think my cousin Clare is the best Armenian cook in the whole DC-Maryland-Virginia area." She grinned. "But I'm the second best. Would you care to sample my talents?"

He gave her a sly, rakish smile. "Baby, I'd love to sample your talents."

"I meant my culinary talents, you dope."

"Oh." He pretended to be disappointed. "When? This Saturday?"

She already had a tentative date, which she knew she was going to break. "Saturday would be fine."

Four

When was the last time she'd taken this much time and trouble to dress for a date? Sharla wondered as she discarded yet another outfit—her seventh—and searched her closet again. Case was due in fifteen minutes and she still hadn't found anything in her wardrobe to her liking. Her makeup was already applied, her thick, glossy hair had been shampooed and brushed until it shone, and the dinner was prepared, with the exception of a few last-minute touches. Now, if she could only make up her mind what to wear . . . She'd certainly had no trouble deciding what *not* to wear. Virtually everything she owned.

In desperation she padded into the small bedroom currently occupied by her cousin Beth. "Feel free to borrow anything of mine that you want, Sharla," Beth had called as she'd left earlier this evening to go out on her own date. Sharla smiled wryly. That was definitely a subtle hint from her young cousin that she considered Sharla's eminently practical wardrobe not quite up to a date with Dr. Casey Flynn.

She surveyed the contents of Beth's closet with a

frown. Beth dressed like a trendy twenty-one-year-old. If there was an item in her cousin's wardrobe for a mature, thirty-year-old woman, she'd yet to run across it.

She glanced at her watch again, and in desperation snatched a periwinkle-blue jumpsuit from a hanger. It was made of a soft, silky material and zipped up the front. So easy to slip out of . . .

The thought popped into Sharla's head and she felt her face grow warm. Case was coming to have dinner, she reminded herself. And the *pahklava* was the dessert, not Sharla Shakarian. She and Case were friends, not lovers. "Friends," she said aloud, and the sound of her voice echoed mockingly in her ears.

Time was running out, and the jumpsuit seemed to be her choice. But to stave off any other wanton thoughts, she avoided slipping the silky garment over her lacy ecru bra and briefs. She added panty hose and a blue-and-white striped cotton turtleneck first. And then was careful to pull the long zipper almost up to her chin. She slipped into a dainty pair of comfortable black flats, affixed small silver hoops to her earlobes, and glanced at her reflection in the mirror once again. She was acting more like twenty than thirty, she told herself. A chastising thought. She walked determinedly away from the mirror, resisting an urge to comb her hair one last time.

Her heart lurched at the sound of the doorbell. The small mantel clock struck eight o'clock. Case was exactly on time. Taking a deep breath, Sharla opened the door.

She almost forgot to exhale as her eyes focused on Case lounging against the door frame. He was tall, dark, and sexy in well-fitting black cords, a black sweater with thin blue lines woven into the fabric, and loafers without socks. "Hello, Sharla." His voice was deep and low and intimate, and his eyes appraised her with a fixed intensity.

"You're right on time," she said brightly, trying

to ignore the tidal wave of sexual awareness sweeping over her.

"You were afraid I'd be late?" He sauntered inside,
all arrogant, uncompromising male. He was fully
aware of the sensual impact he'd had on her, Sharla
knew. That masculine gleam in his eyes, that
satisfied, slightly mocking smile of his . . .

"This is for you." He handed her a box wrapped
in red-and-white paper.

Chocolates, she guessed. "Thank you, Case."
Her fingers shook a little as she took it. Tonight,
Case wasn't the vulnerable, lonely man who'd confided in her. That was the man she'd invited to dinner, but the one who'd just walked in was the
Predatory Wolf-on-the-Make. She watched him eye
the long, wide green sofa, saw his slow, heavy-
lidded smile.

She sighed. "You look like the fox checking out the
chicken coop. Is it going to be *that* kind of evening?"

She had the satisfaction of catching him off
guard. Case stared at her. "What kind of evening?"

"Don't waste your time plotting your moves,
Case," she advised. "You were invited for an Armenian dinner, nothing else."

"Nothing else?" he walked toward her, and she
summoned up every ounce of willpower she possessed to keep from retreating, even a step.

"Nothing else!"

He stood directly in front of her, so close that she
could feel the heat emanating from his hard frame.
"You're dressed for something else besides dinner,
honey." Color flooded her cheeks, and he grinned.
"The jumpsuit." His fingers went to the zipper.
"Such a provocative item of feminine apparel.
Whenever a woman wears it, a man can be certain
that she's imagined him lowering the zipper . . ."

He proceeded to do just that. "Case!" Sharla
grabbed his hand. "Stop it!" Her face was scarlet.
He'd not only guessed her secret fantasy, he was all
set to act it out! She muttered a few choice Armenian words.

He laughed. "Stop swearing at me in Armenian." His other hand slipped behind her back and smoothed the length of her body from her shoulders to her hips. "A few pointers for next time, honey. You've got too many clothes on under the suit. The turtleneck, for one." He traced the outline of her bra with his fingertips. "And underwear."

Before she could move away, his nimble fingers had lowered to the line of her panties. "Good Lord, and panty hose too? Sweetie, you're supposed to be naked under this thing."

She pulled away from him. "Naked?" Her eyes widened. "Do you mean you've been out with a woman who actually wore a jumpsuit with *nothing* under it?"

He grinned rakishly. "More times than I care to count."

"Of course." She frowned. "I'd almost forgotten who I was dealing with—the Olympian of Sex himself."

"Relax, sweetie, no need to feel defensive. I fully understand everything your invitation tonight implies."

"Terrific." She grimaced. "Maybe you'll explain to me what my invitation implies besides sampling a variety of Armenian dishes."

"You're the Armenian dish I'd most like to sample."

"I saw that one coming." She rolled her eyes heavenward. "Sorry to disappoint you, Flynn, but I'm not on the menu."

His dark brows drew together in a frown. "Sharla, no woman invites a man to dinner in her apartment on a Saturday night without making plans for *after* dinner."

"So, it's going to be that kind of evening after all. With you continually alluding to sex and putting the moves on me." She sighed and ran her fingers through her hair, tousling it. "Frankly, Case, I'm not up to it. I was at the hospital till past noon today, then I rushed around like a maniac shopping and cooking for this meal. If I have to spend the rest of the evening fighting you off, I'd rather end it right now."

"End it?" He looked genuinely confused. "I know you want me, Sharla. And you know I want you. Why did you invite me to your apartment if you weren't planning on going to bed with me?"

She gave her head a slight shake. "I know this is going to strike you as incredibly off-the-wall, Case, but I wanted to spend some time with you. I wanted to have dinner and talk and laugh, and maybe even kiss a few times. But that's all."

"Sounds dull. Not my sort of Saturday night date at all."

"Yes, well, there you have it. Take it or leave it."

Therein lay the trap, Case thought. He scowled. If he left, he'd spend the rest of the evening wanting to be here. With Sharla. He could go through every name in his little black book, but he knew there wasn't a woman in it who could serve as an adequate substitute for Sharla Shakarian. It was a chilling thought.

He was caught in a no-win situation. For if he stayed . . . He knew he was running a dangerous course. Spending time with Sharla was not a cure for this absurd infatuation he'd developed for her. It merely seemed to heighten his addiction. The more he saw her, the more he wanted to see her. And after their talk in the hospital cafeteria the other day, that wanting had begun to border alarmingly on needing.

"I have to check on the chicken," Sharla said. She turned and walked out of the room, leaving Case alone to mull over his dilemma. He heard the oven door open, and seconds later a tantalizing aroma wafted into the room. He'd never had Armenian food, he reminded himself. And whatever she was cooking certainly smelled more appealing than anything he'd find in a cardboard box in the freezer compartment of his refrigerator.

Setting his jaw, he strode into the kitchen. "I've decided to stay," he announced. "But strictly for the food."

Sharla, busy at the stove, didn't turn around. "Okay."

"I mean it, Sharla. The only reason I'm staying is because I'm curious to try Armenian food. I like sampling different cuisines. You can ask anyone who knows me and they'll tell you. I'm always game to try some new foreign restaurant."

Sharla suppressed a smile. "I'll take your word for it."

Almost angrily, he crossed the kitchen and caught her by her shoulders, whirling her around to face him. "Dammit, do you understand what I'm saying?"

She nodded, her big ebony eyes alight with amusement. "I understand perfectly, Case. You're telling me that I shouldn't think that your staying for dinner has anything to do with me personally. It's not my company you're staying for, it's the food. You wouldn't give me a thought if you left now, but you would regret missing the chance to have a bona fide Armenian meal."

"That's right," he said crossly. "You've got it, baby."

"I've been told I'm a quick study."

He glared at her. "You're laughing at me!"

"I'm not." She had to look away to conceal her grin.

"Yes, you are. Your eyes are laughing." He caught her chin and forced her to look at him.

She gazed into the stormy blue depths of his eyes and her laughter abruptly faded. Just as Case's burst of anger did. They stared at each other for a long moment. The sexual tension crackled palpably between them.

"I think I'm going to have to," Case murmured, drawing her close.

A dizziness swept over her, leaving her strangely passive and weak. So passive and weak that she seemed unable to do anything but cling to him, waiting for his hard mouth to descend. But the moment his lips touched hers, all passivity fled. Her lips parted and she was kissing him just as wildly as he was kissing her.

His tongue drove deeply into her mouth and she met it with her own. She arched against him, fitting her soft curves into the hard planes of his body. They seemed a perfect fit, two complementing pieces of a well-made puzzle. Two halves joined to form a whole.

They were both so intensely absorbed in each other and the storm of passion that encompassed them that it took a while for the buzz of the oven timer to penetrate their love-drugged senses. But the timer buzzed on, noisily and insistently, and at last, slowly, reluctantly, Case and Sharla surfaced.

She moved to draw back, but he wouldn't let her go. He held her tightly against him, enfolding her in a possessive, protective embrace. The buzz echoed in his ears. "What the hell's *that*?" he asked dazedly.

"The oven timer." She stood on tiptoe to kiss his cheek gently. "The casserole is ready to come out."

He released her, watching as she opened the oven door and removed the casserole dish. His body was throbbing with heat and a hunger totally unrelated to food. He wanted her so badly he ached. Every masculine instinct he possessed screamed for him to grab her and carry her off to bed. Why shouldn't he? he argued with himself. For all her talk, Sharla wanted to be there as much as he did. Her instant, incendiary response to his kiss proved that.

She set the dish on the counter, her whole body trembling with the force of her arousal. "Case," she said so softly that he could barely hear. "I—I'm sorry. You . . . have every right to be furious with me." Her small white teeth sank into her lower lip and she turned to face him. "I seem to say one thing to you and do another. It's not at all like me," she added with a mirthless laugh. "My only excuse is that I—you—" She gulped. "You make me feel things that I've never felt before. When you touch me, I forget everything. I—I just can't seem to think at all."

Case stared at her, floored by her frank admission. He felt much the same way, but he certainly wasn't about to actually *admit* it to her! Revealing such a weakness was merely setting oneself up to be taken advantage of.

Sharla read the incredulity in his eyes. He thought she was a fool to admit her vulnerability to him. Yet somehow acknowledging the sexual power he held over her gave her a little of her own back. She turned her full attention to the salad she was preparing. "I guess you have this effect on a lot of women," she said lightly, and it hurt her to admit that she was one of the legions he had sexually dazzled. But Sharla had never been one to wrap herself in self-delusion. She faced facts and went on from there.

"I guess I do." He smiled his smooth-operator smile, the smile that alternately amused and enraged Sharla. This time, it hurt her. He was special to her, but to him she was indistinguishable from his countless other conquests.

Case saw the shadow flicker in her dark velvet eyes. He drew in his breath sharply. "I have that effect on other women, but you're the only woman who has ever sparked it in me, Sharla."

He was totally disconcerted by what he'd said. He couldn't begin to explain what had made him blurt out his thoughts. Something to do with the momentary sadness in her beautiful eyes, but he pushed that idea away. He was all ready to recall his remark, to make a caustic joke, when Sharla diverted him by changing the subject completely.

"How's Mrs. Aiello?" she asked, tossing the salad with a wooden fork and spoon. "Is she still making progress?"

He eagerly launched into a discussion of his star

patient. "She's doing great! She's off the respirator, and though we still have her on the critical list, she's out of danger. We'll upgrade her condition to serious at the beginning of next week."

"How are her children holding up?" Sharla asked, remembering Case's admiration for the Aiello family.

"I told Mary Margaret she should be proud of the way they all supported each other through all this, sisters, brothers, husbands, wives. They're all so good to each other."

"It sounds as if Mary Margaret and her husband did a fine job raising them."

"They sure did. It must be amazing for her to see these strong, caring adults and remember back to when they were just little kids, to be able to see how well her efforts paid off."

Sharla smiled. "Being a successful parent must be one of the most awesome and rewarding feelings in the world."

"Yes." Case looked thoughtful. "Yes, it must be."

She waited for him to make some distancing wisecrack, but he didn't. Still, another change of subject was definitely in order. Funny how she instinctively knew when to draw back so he wouldn't feel emotionally cornered. "If you'll carry the vegetable tureen to the table, we're ready to eat."

The meal was especially delicious. Case raved over every dish. The chicken in its sauce of walnuts and peppers, the rice pilaf, the chick-peas mixed with sesame seeds. The *soujouk*, or spiced sausage, and *lavash*, a kind of flat bread. And the *pahklava* for dessert. It consisted of honey, nuts, and thin layers of pastry.

"This is baklava," Case said, and Sharla shot him a fierce look.

"It's *pahklava*," she corrected him firmly. "Baklava is Turkish. Enough said!"

"I'll keep that in mind." He chuckled. "And,

Sharla, I don't believe that your cousin Clare is the best Armenian cook in the DC area. I think you are."

They did the dishes together, in a manner of speaking. Sharla washed while Case complained at the number of pots and pans. Occasionally, he dried one. The rest of the time he tried to divert her from the sink by flicking soap bubbles at her, snapping the dish towel, wrapping his arms around her waist, and nibbling on her neck. . . .

She finally gave up and turned in his arms, lifting her face for his kiss. It was long and slow and deep, with all the compelling passion that always flared between them. Yet there was tenderness, too, a tenderness that fueled the hunger into desperate urgency.

Sharla was lost. A wild explosion of voracious passion transformed her into a mindless wanton who could no longer think, but only feel and want and need. Yet it was so much more than mere physical lust. She wanted to give Case all the love and strength within her, as well as fulfill the passionate demands he was making on her. She'd never experienced this strange dichotomy of passion which made her greedy and generous at the same time!

"Oh, Case." She whispered his name on a sigh as she buried her face in the soft material of his sweater. She could hear the strong pounding of his heart beneath her ear. She was trembling, so shaken and aroused by the force of her emotions that she could hardly stand. Her arms tightened around him and she snuggled closer, wanting him, needing him . . . loving him? The thought electrified her. Falling in love with Case Flynn had to head the list of the most foolhardy emotional risks a woman could take. Yet it seemed that Sharla Shakarian, known for her sound judgment and exceptional intuition in medical matters, was on the verge of doing just that.

Case held her, caressing her, kissing the curve of

her neck, inhaling the fragrance of her shiny, ink-black hair. She was deeply aroused, he thought. She was feeling close to him both physically and emotionally, and he knew from past experience with other women that the time was right for him to talk her into bed with a few well-chosen romantic phrases.

So why didn't he say them? Why did he stand in silence, holding her as if he'd never let go? He wanted her so much it hurt. *So why didn't he make his move?*

If he wanted her, she was his, Sharla decided dizzily. She couldn't hold out against the force of her own deepest feelings. She drew back a little and smiled up at him, the message shining in her eyes.

Her smile was so warm and tender it took his breath away. And Case knew in a flash of insight why he wouldn't take advantage of her weakness and rush her into bed. *When you touch me, I forget everything. I just can't seem to think at all.* Her words echoed in his head, and they explained everything. She'd touched him by admitting her vulnerability; she'd aroused his protective instincts. He wanted to protect her from herself, from himself, even if it meant thwarting his own physical desires.

And there was more. He didn't want to seduce Sharla, the past master of seduction realized with a jolt. He wanted her to come to him completely willing and aware, not blinded by manipulation and seduction. He didn't want any regrets or accusations afterward. For the first time ever, he wasn't satisfied with the prospect of sex for its own sake. He wanted mutual respect and caring and . . .

Case abruptly dropped his arms and moved away from her with the speed of a SWAT team moving in on an urban guerilla. Sharla was baffled by his retreat. She'd understood his pulling away when she'd gotten too close emotionally, but she'd been about to surrender physically.

She followed him into the living room, where he stood in the middle of the room looking thoroughly disconcerted. "I don't know whether to go or stay," he said bluntly. "Why don't you make it easier on both of us, Sharla? Kick me out."

"I probably should at that," she said dryly. She'd just made Hospital Center history—the first woman to have her offer of sex turned down by Casey Flynn. She reached for the gift he'd given her on his arrival. "I forgot to open the candy you brought me," she said absently, and quickly tore off the paper. She was relieved to have something to do to break the awkward tension between them.

"Uh, it isn't candy," Case said rather sheepishly.

She stared at the box she held in her hands. No, it wasn't candy. It was a game. "Sexual Trivia," she said, and quickly opened the lid. Inside was a playing board, plastic pieces and—"Four sex manuals?" she asked. Her eyes widened as she leafed through Sex Manual One. "Test your knowledge of sexual awareness and erotica," she read, and then gasped. "Good grief, it says here that—"

Case snatched the manual away from her. "It seemed like a good idea at the time." He shrugged. "An inventive addition to foreplay."

Sharla was glancing through Sex Manual Two. "Do you want to play a few rounds?"

"No. You don't need any additional foreplay. If I get you any hotter, you'll burst into flames."

She met his gaze steadily. "Is that why you ran away from me? Because you were afraid of getting burned?"

"I didn't run away from you." He felt a flush start at his neck and spread up to his face. "I . . . uh, was assailed by some stupid, misguided notion of chivalry. But I didn't run away!"

Clearly, she'd struck a nerve. "You were protecting me? Is that what you're trying to say?"

He scowled. "Why do you always want everything

spelled out for you? All right, dammit, yes! I was protecting you."

"Well, you don't have to protect me, not even from myself." A reckless excitement ricocheted through her, and her black eyes were bright with daring. "I'm a big girl, Case. I make my own decisions and I'm willing to take whatever consequences follow."

"Are you, Sharla?" His whole body reacted to her challenge. He reached out to grab her hand. She jerked it away from him, her gaze holding his, deliberately provocative. "Are you really?"

She smiled, daring him, tempting him, maddening him. "Yes."

"Then let's see what happens when you take me on, sweetheart." He made another snatch for her hand, and this time he caught it. With one strong tug, he pulled her to him.

His mouth lowered to hers as she raised her face to him. And at that fateful moment the apartment door opened and Beth and Alex Shakarian walked in.

"Consider yourself saved, lady," Case said in a low voice.

"Consider *yourself* saved, mister," Sharla said, her eyes never leaving his.

"Oh, Sharla, I'm so sorry to interrupt!" Beth exclaimed. "But my date got drunk as a skunk at the party and then insisted that he wanted to go out on the town. He was in absolutely no shape to drive, so I got his keys away from him and called Alex, and he came and took us both home." She pulled a set of keys out of her purse. "Just in case he feels like going for a little ride tonight, I kept his keys."

"Hmm, another scheming Shakarian woman." Case glared from Sharla to Beth. Sweet little Beth, he thought, was going to be as dangerous to some poor unsuspecting male someday as her cousin Sharla was to him.

"You did exactly the right thing, Bethy," Sharla said. "I'm proud of you."

"But I'm awfully sorry we crashed your evening," Beth said. "Sharla cooked Case an Armenian dinner," she explained to Alex.

"Any leftovers, Sharla?" Alex was already heading for the kitchen.

"Plenty," Sharla called after him. "Help yourself."

"I think I will too," Beth said. "I didn't get much to eat at the party." She joined Alex in the kitchen.

Sharla turned to Case. "I guess you'll be on your way." He'd made it extremely clear how he felt about mingling with family.

"And have you accuse me of running away?" he replied coolly. "You're not winning this round, honey. I'm staying. I don't mind putting up with your kid cousins for a while."

He ended up staying for another three hours. And he did more than merely "put up" with the cousins' company. All four of them talked—Hospital Center gossip mostly—then Alex began asking Case questions about the Shock/Trauma Unit.

"I have an externship next summer before my senior year," he said, "and I'd really like to do it on the ST Unit. Trauma surgery is what I'd like to specialize in. But I hear that Jake Schroeder doesn't like med students hanging around."

"He makes a few exceptions," Case said. He didn't add that the exceptions were those students who were sponsored by a high-ranking member of the staff. He didn't have to. All of them understood the system.

Alex wisely let the subject drop. "Can I have some more *pahklava*, Sharla?" He grinned good-naturedly. "It's as good as Grandma's."

Sharla beamed. "For that you can have a double portion, darling boy."

The four of them launched into a game of Sexual Trivia and played several rounds, howling with laughter at the frank questions and answers. And at the unexpected outcome of the game.

"I can't believe it," Case said with a mock gasp. "*Beth* had a higher score than I did? Sweet, innocent little Beth beat the Big Bad Wolf?" His eyes connected with Sharla's.

"Maybe you're not such a Big Bad Wolf after all," she said airily. "Maybe you're really a lamb in wolf's clothing."

"Please, don't tamper with the legend!" Alex pleaded jokingly. "Let the myth of Casey Flynn live on!"

"You tell 'em, kid," said Case, laughing. "Listen, Alex, page me on Monday and I'll see about arranging a tour of the unit for you. Maybe if I introduce you to Jake and let him see that you're no threat to his mental health, you might even get that externship."

"Thanks, Case!" Alex was thrilled. Neither he nor Sharla were fooled by Case's seeming nonchalance. They all knew that if Case Flynn asked the director to allow an extern on the Shock/Trauma Unit, the externship was as good as in the bag.

Sharla wondered about that as she stared at Case. Why was he going to use his influence to get Alex a position on the STU? Case Flynn was not the mentor type. Was he, by any chance, motivated by the fact that Alex was her cousin?

Alex left shortly afterward, and Beth went to her room. Sharla walked Case to the door.

"Don't," he warned, looking down at her.

"Don't what?"

"Don't look at me that way." Her dark eyes were soft with love, her face radiant. Case felt a sharp, sudden shaft of fear. "Sharla, we should stop seeing each other."

She put her arms around him and laid her head against his hard chest. "Why?" Her hands rubbed his back with slow, gentle strokes.

"I'm going to hurt you," he said hoarsely. "It's

inevitable, Sharla. And I—don't want to see you get hurt."

"You don't have to worry about me," she said. "I can take care of myself. I'm a survivor, Case. All the Shakarians are. We were raised to be. When our grandparents survived the massacre, they were determined that their progeny would be strong and carry on for all those who didn't make it. 'Don't run from life, run out and embrace it,' my grandfather has always said." She silently substituted *love* for *life*. Weren't the two almost interchangeable, anyway?

Case drew a deep breath. The touch, the feel of her was going straight to his head like a shot of the most potent brandy. "This conversation is bordering on the surrealistic." He gave a slight laugh. "I try to warn you to stay away from me, and you quote a chapter in Armenian history."

"We're a strange pair," she agreed cheerfully.

They held each other in silence as seconds ticked by.

"About tomorrow," Case began, and Sharla's heart leaped for joy. She'd fully expected him to leave without making any mention of seeing her again. She'd expected him to keep "casually" running into her at the hospital for a long while before he got around to making definite plans to see her.

"I promised my little sister I'd go to her house for dinner tomorrow," he said. "I've only seen my new nephew once since he was born, and Shay let me know that she's not very pleased that I've shirked my avuncular duties."

"Shirking avuncular duties? Shame on you, Case! You'd better spend the afternoon with your nephews to make amends."

"I'm not too big on family togetherness. I usually arrive an hour before dinner and stay for an hour afterward. That's all Shay expects. Would . . . uh, you care to come along? I know visiting relatives is tedious and I know I didn't go to your family birthday dinner, and—"

"I'll go with you," Sharla interrupted before he talked himself into withdrawing the invitation. "I'm used to visiting relatives. I did it every Sunday while I was growing up."

"You have my heartfelt sympathy." He moved away from her and opened the door. "I'll pick you up tomorrow shortly after four."

"I'll be ready," she said softly. "Good night, Case."

He took a step out the door, then turned and grabbed her, pulling her close. He kissed her, hard, then released her abruptly and dashed out of the apartment.

Sharla stared after him, gazing dreamily into space.

"Sharla?"

The sound of her name slowly penetrated the sensual fog. Beth had come into the room and was watching Sharla, who was staring out into the empty hall. Flushing, Sharla quickly closed the door and tried to look sensible.

Beth smiled. "I think Case is really nice, Sharla. And now that I've spent some time with him, I don't think all those stories about him are true."

"You mean the tales of his legendary love life? I think most of them are, Beth."

"Oh, well, then maybe he's turned over a new leaf. You know, Grandpa always says that no one is beyond redemption. Sharla, I can't wait for the family back in Racine to meet him!"

Sharla tried and failed to imagine Case meeting the huge Shakarian clan en masse in Racine. She was a realist, after all. "Case isn't a marrying man, Beth," she told her cousin as she reminded herself of the fact. "He's not going to meet the family back in Racine."

"But the man's crazy about you!" Beth argued.

Sharla felt a syrupy warmth flow through her. She was more than a little crazy about Case. But that was much too private to discuss. "Good night, Beth," she said pointedly, and started to walk out of the room. When Beth began to warble an Armenian love song, Sharla snatched a throw pillow from the chair and threw it at her, laughing in spite of herself.

Five

Sharla was stretched out on the living room carpet, constructing a wall out of plastic blocks so Scotty Wickwire, Case's two-year-old nephew, could crash a toy car into it and knock it over. A molded figure of Cookie Monster rode shotgun in the tiny wooden vehicle, and every time the blocks collapsed Scotty shrieked, "Get cookies," and screamed in delight, captivated by his own wit.

It was a great game for a two-year-old and Scotty loved it so much he insisted that Sharla play it over and over. She really didn't mind. She enjoyed children, and didn't get to see much of her own nieces, nephews, and small cousins these days. And she was dressed casually in green corduroy slacks and a pink, yellow, and green sweater, suitable clothes for romping on the floor.

Sharla liked the Wickwires—Case's "little sister" Shay, a pretty, blue-eyed, dark-haired young woman; her attorney husband, Adam; and their two little boys, the effervescent Scotty and month-old Brandon, who spent most of the visit snoozing in a wicker bassinet in a corner of the spacious liv-

ing room. Shay and Adam were physically affec-
tionate with each other and with their children.
They smiled and laughed a lot and were clearly very
happy. Sharla felt comfortable with them immediately. The Wickwires would have fit easily into the
close, amiable Shakarian clan.

But they made Case and his twin sister Candy
exceedingly nervous. Sharla could feel the under-
current of tension throughout the visit. Both Case
and Candy, a slim and beautiful green-eyed bru-
nette who looked years younger than the forty
Sharla knew her to be, sat on the edges of their
chairs, their gazes flicking from Adam to Shay to
the children, as if waiting . . .

Waiting for what? Sharla wondered. For Shay
and Adam suddenly to begin to snarl and smash
things? Given the Flynns' dismal upbringing, perhaps it was understandable, but Sharla found it
unnerving and depressing. She could imagine how
Shay and Adam felt, being the objects of such pessimistic scrutiny. No wonder the Flynn family vis-
its were short and infrequent!

Yet Shay was eager for family ties. Sharla picked
up on that at once. Shay was warm and welcoming, and unabashedly thrilled that her brother had
brought Sharla along, once she got over the initial
shock of Sharla's unexpected arrival.

Case hadn't bothered to mention to his sisters
that he was bringing a guest. Nor had he bothered
to tell Sharla that she was the first woman he'd
ever asked to meet his family. He didn't have to.
The stunned expressions on Shay's and Candy's
faces when she'd walked in the door had said it all.

Shay, Adam, and the children had accepted
Sharla at once. Not so Candace Flynn. All during
the visit Sharla felt Case's twin studying her with
cool analytic reserve. When Candy directed a few
questions to her in the style of a prosecutor taking
on the defense's star witness, Sharla held her own,
but silently admitted that she would hate to face
the steely-eyed Candace Flynn in a courtroom.

Sharla also noticed that, after having taken the unheard-of step of bringing a woman to meet his family, Case seemed totally at a loss as to what to do with her. So he ignored her. Occasionally he would steal a covert glance, but if either of his sisters caught him looking at Sharla, he would immediately look away, feigning indifference.

Sharla, ever adaptable and gregarious, quickly made herself at home. Soon it seemed as if *she* were Shay and Adam's relative. She chatted easily with the couple, played with the children, and helped with the dinner while Case and Candy observed in detached silence.

There was a brief, relaxed period when Adam took Case to his wine cellar and Sharla tagged along. Both Adam and Case were avid wine buffs, and indulged in a good-natured debate about German wines—Adam's preference—versus French wines—Case's choice.

"What about you, Sharla?" Adam asked, turning to her. "Which do you prefer?"

About the only thing Sharla knew about wines was that some were red and some were white. "I like California Coolers," she said.

Case and Adam exchanged appalled glances. "Get her out of my wine cellar," Adam said jokingly.

"Glad to oblige," Case said, grinning. "What a little philistine!" In one easy movement he swung Sharla over his shoulder in a fireman's hold and started out the door. Candy and Shay were coming in. Case took one look at his sisters and nearly dropped Sharla on her head. He didn't go near her for the rest of the evening.

Baby Brandon awakened at a few minutes past seven and Sharla asked to hold him. Shay proudly deposited her infant son in Sharla's arms.

"He's such a strong, sturdy baby," Sharla said, cuddling the child. "Both your children are beautiful, Shay."

"We've been very lucky," Shay said softly, casting

a warm glance at her husband, who was reading a storybook to a sleepy-eyed Scotty.

Case stood up and announced abruptly, "It's time for me to leave."

Candy also rose. "I have to be running along too."

"First let me dress the baby in the little suit that Sharla brought him so she can see him in it," Shay said. "Come up to the nursery with me, Sharla."

Sharla saw Case and Candy exchange glances. "Do you mind if we stay a few minutes longer, Case?" she asked.

He frowned and glanced at his watch. "No more than five minutes."

"It'll take longer than five minutes to change and dress the baby." Sharla smiled sweetly. "Would you rather leave immediately, Case? I can always get a taxi home."

He sat down. "Ten more minutes," he said stiffly. "Not a second longer."

"Can't you read the handwriting on the wall, brother?" Candy said, and laughed. A not altogether pleasant laugh. "You'll leave when Sharla's good and ready to leave and not a second before."

"Let's go upstairs," Shay said quickly. She hurried from the room, the baby in her arms. Sharla followed at a leisurely pace, pausing to stroke Case's shoulder. He flushed and quickly shifted away from her. Shay watched from the staircase.

"I—I really feel I should apologize for my sister and brother's behavior today," Shay said as she led Sharla into little Brandon's bright green-and-yellow nursery. "They've barely spoken to you, and that little scene downstairs just now . . ." She sighed.

"No apology is necessary," Sharla said. "I understand Case well enough to know that he's regretting bringing me here today. But I'm glad he did, Shay. I've thoroughly enjoyed meeting you and Adam and the children."

"It was a pleasure having you. You lightened up

the atmosphere considerably." Shay grimaced wryly. "Perhaps you noticed that Case and Candy spent the entire visit waiting for Adam and me to start brawling or tossing the children out the windows or something equally violent."

"Is it always that way?" Sharla asked gently.

"Always. Adam and I joke about it, but it's really not funny." Shay's blue eyes sought Sharla's. "Adam and I have a good marriage. We rarely fight, and when we do, there certainly isn't any violence. We've never hurt the children and we never will. Why can't Case and Candy accept the idea that a family can live happily together?"

"Sometimes people find new ideas more threatening than their safe, old fixed ones." Sharla laid her finger in the baby's palm and his tiny fingers reflexively gripped it. "Case and Candy equate family life with pain. From their point of view, it's much easier to pretend love just isn't possible, I suppose."

"I grew up idolizing Case and Candy. But since I married Adam, I've grown away from them," Shay said sadly. "I just can't accept their cynicism. Or their pessimism." She carefully dressed the baby in Sharla's gift to him, a red, white, and blue velour stretch suit. "Please don't give up on my brother, Sharla! He needs someone like you so much. He's so alone, and I want him to be happy, as happy and fulfilled as I am."

"Ten minutes are up. We're leaving, Sharla." Case appeared in the doorway of the nursery, his expression dark and brooding. He turned and headed down the stairs without a backward glance.

"We *will* see you again," Shay insisted, hugging Sharla quickly as they stood on the doorstep. Case shifted impatiently from one foot to the other, then stalked off to his car.

"Go ahead and say it," Sharla said to him as the

Lotus roared down the Wickwires' long driveway into the quiet streets of Potomac, Maryland.

"Say what?" Case snapped.

"What you're dying to say. That if I ever see Shay and Adam again, it will be strictly on my own because *you're* certainly not going to have any part in it."

"That's true," he said between clenched teeth.

"And tell me what a big mistake you made, introducing me to your sisters."

"It was a mistake, all right. I overheard Shay begging you to stick with me because I'm so alone. Well, you don't have to do me any favors, lady. I'm alone because I want to be."

"Of course you are!" Sharla agreed heartily. "And don't be angry with Shay. Being meddlesome on a family member's behalf is perfectly normal and understandable. No one knows that better than I."

"Will you kindly stop placating me? I find it insulting."

"Sorry. Let's see, where were we? Oh, yes, we were talking about how sorry you are that you invited me to meet your family."

"You're damn right I'm sorry!"

Sharla settled back in her seat with a knowing smile. "Now that we have that out of the way, I want to say that I liked Shay and Adam very much and that their babies are adorable. I had a wonderful time visiting them."

"I'm glad *you* did." Case was determined to sink into a moody silence, but she wouldn't let him, dammit. He scowled. The afternoon had been a disaster from the moment he'd walked into his sister's house and seen Candy and Shay go nearly catatonic with shock at the sight of Sharla. He heartily regretted his impulsive invitation to her. Whatever could have prompted him to issue it, anyway?

Sharla had fit in so easily, so effortlessly with Shay and Adam, he thought. She was wonderful with the children. And the sight of her with the baby in her arms had set off alarm bells in his head. She looked absolutely right holding the blue-eyed baby boy. Little Brandon Wickwire had his uncle Case's light-blue eyes. He looked very much like a son of Casey Flynn's might look. And seeing the child in Sharla's arms . . .

No! he assured himself. Mid-life crisis, biological forces, whatever was inducing this absurd sentimentality, he wasn't going to get caught in *that* trap as others before him had—his father, a number of friends, his brother-in-law . . . "Shay was pregnant when she married Adam," he said suddenly, sharply. "Scotty was born five months after his parents were married."

"Am I supposed to have an attack of the vapors or something?" Sharla asked, and shrugged. "So what?"

"Sharla, Shay deliberately planned to get pregnant. Adam was literally trapped into marrying her."

"Baloney! A woman doesn't get pregnant by herself, mister. There's a wonderful old cliché that goes 'It takes two to tango,' if you get my drift." Sharla's dark eyes flashed. "Anyway, the current reality is that Shay and Adam are happily married and successfully raising a family. And you can't stand it, can you, Casey Flynn? Your little sister has shot your theory full of holes and you keep looking for ways to make it whole again."

"You're such a bitch," Case said, almost with wonderment.

"And you're such a blockhead. No wonder we get along so well."

"What does it take to get you upset?" Case sighed with exasperation. "I ignore you the entire time we're at my sister's, I glare at you and snap at you and insult you. Why, any other woman would be—"

"Weeping or raging?" Sharla supplied helpfully.

"Yes! But it all simply bounces off you."

"I save my tears and rage for things that really matter, Case." Sharla was suddenly serious. "For babies who die because they were born too small and too soon, for the cruelties and injustices one group of people perpetrates against another. A petty little lovers' quarrel seems terribly insignificant compared to all that."

They rode in silence the rest of the way to Sharla's apartment. Case pulled the Lotus into the parking space beside her little gray CRX. She unlocked the door and was opening it when Case reached across her and pulled it shut. He pulled her roughly into his arms, as if he expected her to resist. She didn't; she went to him willingly. He needed to hold her as much as she needed to be held.

"A lovers' quarrel, hmm?" he said, resuming the conversation as if they hadn't been silent for the past forty minutes. "So you're already thinking of us as lovers, are you? May I remind you that we're *not* lovers, as we've never been to bed."

"It was merely a figure of speech," she said a bit too breathlessly to pull off the bright insouciance she was striving for.

"No." His eyes were level with hers, and she felt herself being drawn into them by the magnetic force of his gaze. "We're definitely going to be lovers. It's merely a matter of when I decide to take you to bed, my little torment."

"When *you* decide? Don't I have a say in the matter?" Her heartbeat had already begun to speed up. Her mouth was suddenly dry, and she moistened her lips with her tongue, the nervous gesture unconsciously provocative. She laid her head back in the curve of his arm and gazed up at him.

"Suppose I said you had no choice whatsoever?" he asked quietly. "What would you do if I were to say something like 'we both know I can have you whenever I feel like taking you'?"

She could feel the tension within him. The hard muscles of his body were as taut as a coiled spring. "Is that the kind of arrogant, macho remark you've made in the past when a woman started getting too close?" she asked carefully. "When you found your-self liking her or wanting her too much?"

Case said nothing, but his arms tightened around her, as if he were holding on to her despite the conflicting urge to force her away. Sharla was filled with an overwhelming rush of compassion for him. How terrible to be at war with yourself! To come within reach of what you want and need, only to feel compelled to thrust it away.

"I can guess what happens after you say some-thing like that," she continued softly. "The pure male arrogance inflames the woman and stirs up a fairly primitive female response. She does some-thing like slap your face—"

"Or tries to," Case amended.

"Yes, you'd see a slap coming, wouldn't you? So you'd grab her arm and then you'd probably scuffle a little . . . Have I got it right so far?"

"Perfectly," he said grimly.

"And you and I both know how loathsome you find physical violence." She gazed directly into his eyes, not letting him look away. "Unfortunately, your sparring partner wouldn't know because you'd never mentioned your parents' terrible fights to her. So she's been set up. To her, your little physical tussle is sexually exciting. After all, you're not hurting her and she's not afraid of you. But to you, it means that she's capable of inciting you to react violently. I can guess what happens next."

"The little tussle inevitably leads to lovemaking," he said. "She surrenders completely. Then I break off at a crucial moment and say something like, 'I told you I could have you whenever I want you. And I've decided I don't want you right now. Maybe I will in an hour, in a day or a week, whenever. All I'll have to do is snap my fingers, and you'll come running.'"

Case averted his eyes. Lord, how many times had he enacted that scene? he wondered. How many times had he coldly steeled himself against the tears and anger that followed? He felt a swift surge of self-dislike.

"No woman with even a modicum of pride could tolerate such treatment," Sharla said. "There's another fight and it's all over. And you tell yourself that you're justified in what you've done. Better to end it immediately than to risk a replay of your parents' horrendous relationship. And the poor woman never knows what happened or why, because she never got a look at the script you forced on her."

Case scowled. "You must have been the shining light of your psych rotation, Dr. Shakarian."

She nodded. "Yes, I was. And I imagine you were like all the aspiring surgeons in my class, who found psychology and anything to do with it boring, useless, and an utter waste of your time. Did you have a bumper sticker on your car saying I'd Rather Be Operating?"

He laughed reluctantly. "I would've if I'd run across one."

"But we're getting off the subject." Sharla cupped the curve of his jaw with her palm and turned his head to her. His blue eyes burned into hers. "Since we've already talked through the Fight/Breakup Scene, can we just skip going through it for real? I probably wouldn't play my part the way you expected me to, anyway."

"No, you probably wouldn't." Case did his best to frown fiercely at her. "At least, not now."

"Poor Case. Now you'll have to come up with a different way to drive me away." Her dark eyes danced mischievously, and she brushed his lips lightly with hers. "Why don't you just save us both a lot of time and effort and admit to yourself that you want me to stick around?"

"Is that what you think?" he growled.

"That's what I know," she said. "You couldn't bring yourself to go through with your standard Fight/Breakup Scene because you don't want to hurt me. You told me that yourself. And I believe you, Casey Flynn. You won't hurt me—you like me too much. And you want me too much.''

"Trust you to bring up everything I've ever said in a weak moment," he groused.

"We shining lights feel an obligation to keep our thickheaded surgeon colleagues psychologically informed." She sat up and straightened her sweater. "It's getting late, Case. I'd better go in."

"It's not even nine o'clock," he protested, and abruptly lapsed into an appalled silence. He'd almost tried to argue her into staying with him! *Because he didn't want her to go.* This was not the way he'd envisioned this evening ending at all. According to the scenario he'd planned at Shay and Adam's this afternoon, he and Sharla were supposed to be through with each other by this time tonight. He had definitely decided to end it with her. Things were getting too complicated, out of hand. The Fight/Breakup Scene had seemed an ideal way to push her out of his life.

But instead of saying the offensive lines, he'd warned her in advance, thus rendering one of his most effective strategies ineffective. If he were to try seriously to enact that scene now, Sharla would undoubtedly dissolve into laughter. Then he'd find himself laughing and . . . He turned his head to find her watching him, her eyes as warm as black velvet.

"You're right," he said thickly. "It is getting late." He quickly got out of the car and came around to her side to open the door.

She tucked her hand in the crook of his elbow as they walked to her apartment door. Once she brushed her cheek against his arm. She loved being with him, she loved touching him, she thought. She was beginning to believe that she loved *him.* And Casey Flynn wasn't an easy man to love. He was complex and cynical, with a fortress around his heart. She wasn't going to have an easy time of it, she realized, suppressing a sigh. But

Case seemed to reach her on so many levels. She'd never felt this way about anyone before.

They stood in the hallway in front of her apartment door. Sharla searched her purse for her keys. Case watched her. He was out of his depth with her, he admitted glumly to himself. He'd never known a woman like her. He'd thought it would never happen to him, but it had. He'd met the woman who could bring him to his knees. The acknowledgment thoroughly unnerved him. And angered him too.

Sharla found her key, inserted it in the door, and opened it. "I had a lovely day. Thanks very much for inviting me, Case." She smiled at him.

The she-devil! he thought. She knew damn well how that smile of hers affected him. "If you're waiting for me to tell you when I'll call you again," he blurted out furiously, "you'll have a long wait."

Her smile broadened. "Good night, Case."

"I've never been one of those lovestruck idiots who calls every day and makes weekend plans a whole week before."

"Me either," she said affably.

"So if you're trying to—to finagle a phone call from me tomorrow, you can just forget it!"

"I wouldn't dream of trying to finagle anything from you, Case." She pressed her fingertips to her lips, then lightly touched them to his mouth. "Good night," she said softly, and stepped inside and closed the door.

For a long moment Case simply stared at the closed door, fighting the awful sense of loss and loneliness welling up within him. Turning rapidly, he stormed down the stairs and out into the cooling September night.

The telephone rang shortly after midnight. Sharla came instantly awake and snatched the receiver from its cradle. "Dr. Shakarian," she said briskly. Mentally, she was already en route to the hospital.

"Did I wake you, Dr. Shakarian?"

She sank back into the pillows. "Yes, you did, Dr. Flynn."

"You mean you weren't lying awake, tossing and turning and wondering when and if you'd ever hear from me again?"

She was never in a particularly good mood when first roused from sleep unless it was a bona fide emergency. Then, of course, she marshaled all her resources into a semblance of amiability.

This did *not* qualify as a bona fide emergency. "Suppose I said I was doing just that?" she snapped. "Would you get off the phone and let me get back to sleep?"

"So the perfect Dr. Shakarian has a flaw, after all. She's a grouch when she first wakes up. Not to mention totally devoid of humor."

"Not to mention that. May I assume that you called for a reason other than to point out my flaws?"

"I wanted to tell you that I was going to be tied up all day tomorrow and couldn't meet you for lunch."

"Good. Because I'm going to be tied up all day tomorrow, too, and I couldn't meet you for lunch either." She paused, confused. "Were we supposed to meet for lunch?"

"No, but I thought you might be hoping that I'd drop by the nursery and suggest it."

She almost laughed. Fortunately, she managed not to. "Well, I'm glad you called to tell me, Case," she said carefully. "That's . . . uh, just what I was hoping."

"No, you weren't!" Case gave an impatient, self-derisive snort. "You weren't thinking of me at all. You were *sleeping*!" He slammed down the receiver.

Sharla winced, his indignant accusation ringing in her ear, along with the ferocious bang of the telephone. She'd always been regarded as an excellent diagnostician, and she was recognizing all the signs. Casey Flynn might not know it yet, but he'd fallen for her—hard. Her mouth curved into a tender little smile. The poor guy. He'd spent a lifetime avoiding it, only to fall in love for the first time at the age of forty. He felt confused, disconcerted, and angry, and she couldn't blame him.

The telephone rang again, and she picked it up. "Hello, Case."

"How did you know it would be me?" he growled.

"I took a wild guess."

"You're taking great delight in this, aren't you, Sharla? In making a fool of me?"

"Case, I'm not making a fool of you," she said patiently.

"No, you don't have to, do you?" He sighed. "I'm doing a spectacular job of it on my own."

"I'm glad you called back, Case." He made no reply. She guessed he was berating himself for calling back. The next move was clearly up to her. "I was wondering if you could meet me for dinner tomorrow night? In the hospital snack bar or cafeteria?"

She found herself holding her breath while he considered it. "I don't know. I'll have to check my schedule," he replied with a cool indifference that sparked her temper. "Call me tomorrow and I'll let you know."

Sharla's temper blazed into a full-fledged conflagration. Dammit, she was too old for these stupid games. She was willing to make allowances for his prickly male ego, but she was nobody's doormat!

"Forget it," she said. "I just checked *my* schedule and *I* can't make it. Some other time, maybe. Give me a call and I'll let you know. Good night, Case." She hung up, punched her pillow, and flopped over onto her stomach, muttering her darkest Armenian curse words.

When the phone rang a half hour later, she was still wide awake. She hoped it was the hospital.

Since sleeping seemed impossible, she might as well be working.

"I didn't wake you this time." There was a smile in Case's voice.

"What do you want *now*?" Her tone was most ungracious.

He cleared his throat. "I . . . uh, checked my schedule and it seems that I'm free to have dinner with you tomorrow night at the snack bar." There was a brief pause. "If you . . . uh, happen to be free, that is."

"Are you asking me to have dinner with you?" she asked sternly.

"No." He couldn't bring himself to admit it. He did *not* have a weakness for her, he reassured himself. "You asked *me* to have dinner with *you*, remember? I'm merely responding to your invitation."

"I canceled the invitation, remember?" Lord, he was stubborn. Sharla scowled. It was the middle of the night and she was in no mood to play one-upmanship games with him. "And that's where we stand right now."

"Don't you want to have dinner with me?"

"Just as much as you want to have dinner with me!"

He laughed suddenly. Sharla could certainly give as well as she got, he thought. There was no doubt about that. "Then meet me at the snack bar at six forty-five tomorrow evening," he said.

"Snack bar. Six forty-five tomorrow evening," she repeated. "Good night, Dr. Flynn."

He was determined to have the last word. "Good night, baby." He'd intended to sound rakish and arrogant. The tender, intimate note in his voice was as big a surprise to him as it must have been to Sharla. He swallowed. "Good night, Sharla." This time his voice was that of a lover, sorry to break the connection that linked him to his beloved. He hadn't intended that, either. Thoroughly spooked, Case hung up the phone.

Six

"Dr. Shakarian, Diane Patterson would like to see you whenever you have a free moment." The nurse from the obstetrical floor approached Sharla just as she was emerging from the Intensive Care Nursery.

Sharla glanced at her watch. "I'll go in and see her now." She was to meet Case in the fifth-floor doctors' lounge in five minutes, but Case understood patient priority, and Diane Patterson was a very special patient. Sharla entered the small private room across the hall from the nurses' station. Since Diane's admission to the maternity floor three weeks ago, she and Sharla had struck up a warm friendship which went beyond their doctor/patient relationship. Sharla made it a point to visit with the thirty-one-year-old woman every day, although the eight babies she carried wouldn't become Sharla's patients until after their birth.

Diane put down the magazine she'd been reading when Sharla walked in the door. "Sharla, I'm sorry to be such a bother. I know we talked earlier today, but—"

"You're no bother," Sharla interrupted firmly. She walked to the edge of the bed and took Diane's hand. Diane's eyes were red-rimmed and her nose was puffy. "You've been crying," Sharla said with a frown of concern.

"J-just an attack of the blues." Diane's eyes filled with tears. "Sharla, I felt some contractions today, strong ones. I told Dr. Knowlton and he didn't seem worried. But then, he'd never let on to me if he *was* worried. He's the calmest man I've ever met."

"He is that." Sharla smiled. "I checked your chart today, Diane. Dr. Knowlton thinks you're simply having uterine contractions due to the increasing size of the uterus. They're perfectly normal and *not* the beginning signs of labor."

Diane clutched Sharla's hand. "Sharla, they can't be born yet, it's still much too soon. I'll—I'll lose them all." Her voice broke on a sob.

"Diane, you're twenty-five weeks along now." Sharla's voice was soft and soothing. "It's true that babies born before the twenty-sixth week are on the edge of viability, but it's not all that rare for them to survive. We had a baby girl born at twenty-four weeks who's a healthy one-year-old today."

"But I'll bet she wasn't one of eight! Oh, Sharla, Don and I want a baby so badly. We'd do anything—"

"You're doing everything you possibly can, Diane. I know how difficult it's been for you to be on complete bed rest for the past three weeks, but you haven't complained once about the boredom and the physical discomfort of carrying eight babies." Sharla leaned over to hug the woman. "And you're going to take a baby home, I promise you. Personally, I think you'll be taking all eight home."

Diane clung to her for a moment. "No, we have no hopes for that. Not after the last time. I'm terrified it'll happen again, Sharla. We'll lose them all. There won't be even one baby for us."

"We're not going to lose them all," Sharla said with forceful conviction. She gazed steadily into Diane's tear-filled eyes. "We're not, Diane." Slowly the tension began to drain from the woman's swollen body.

"You really think so?" Diane whispered.

"Diane, I know so." It was necessary to keep Diane's spirits up, and Sharla always managed to impart the optimism and confidence the frightened mother-to-be needed. The prospect of Diane Patterson losing all her babies was an unthinkable one. Sharla never let herself even consider such a possibility.

Diane was still very much on her mind as Sharla made her way to the fifth-floor lounge to meet Case. He wasn't there when she arrived—no doubt delayed by a patient of his own—so she poured herself a cup of coffee and settled down in a comfortable armchair to wait. Inevitably, her thoughts turned to Case. She seemed to spend most of her free time these days thinking about the man.

She and Case had been seeing each other on an irregularly regular basis for the past three and a half weeks. They'd meet for quick lunches and dinners at the hospital snack bar, fitting them in as their demanding schedules allowed. Occasionally, they would have a "real date," as young Beth called it. That consisted of Case picking Sharla up at her apartment and taking her to a restaurant or perhaps a movie. Never on a weekend, though. The past three weekends had seen a rash of automobile accidents, with Case in surgery till all hours of the night.

Case didn't seem to care for the "real date" format, anyway, Sharla mused. It probably smacked too much of a traditional courtship, which could lead to the ultimate of horrors for him—a commitment. And she was certain he would deny that he talked to her on the phone every day, although he did. She wasn't sure he realized it himself. But he called every night—sometimes early in the evening, sometimes long after she had gone to bed. He never called, of course, for the express purpose of merely talking to her.

She secretly grinned over the assortment of reasons he found to call her. He'd found questions that needed immediate answers involving CRX sports cars, articles in medical journals, trivial hospital news. A few times he'd called to tell her he was not—*absolutely not*—going to call her the next day. Which he would conveniently forget when he called her the next day on some other pretext.

Once on the line, their conversations were inevitably lengthy and interesting, alternately amusing and serious. And revealing. Sharla was certain that Case didn't realize how much of himself he shared with her during those long, lazy telephone conversations. The powerful sexual tension that flared between them when they were together kept him on guard emotionally, but across the telephone wires he could relax and let the barriers down.

Sometimes they discussed their respective patients. They were both in fields involving highly advanced technology, both dealing daily with high-risk situations in which finely honed skills and the intuitive ability to take an innovative chance meant the difference between winning and losing a patient.

It was gratifying to be able to talk to someone who so thoroughly understood the demands and rewards of a highly specialized field, Sharla had thought after she'd confided the news of the unborn octuplets to Case. He was genuinely excited about her upcoming role as their doctor. And though he held a darkly pessimistic view of love and marriage, he was a firm believer in the power of positive thinking when it came to the field of medicine. "You're going to make medical history, Sharla," he insisted when she expressed anxieties about the eight infants' chances. "You're going to pull them through."

Sharla respected him, she admired him, and, most of all, she loved him. What she'd suspected so early in their relationship had been confirmed for her these past weeks. She was in love with Casey Flynn. And though he'd never admitted it—she wondered if he ever would—she believed that he loved her too.

She was ready and willing to give herself completely to the man she loved. What Case had said obliquely, that Sunday night after their visit to Shay and Adam's, was true. *We both know I can have you whenever I feel like taking you.* But he'd never said it again, not even obliquely, and he'd never acted upon it either. Passion simmered between them in their most casual touches and gazes. It burst into flames when they kissed. But time and opportunity to move beyond kisses continued to elude them. Their professional demands aside, Beth was ever present in Sharla's apartment. And Case had yet to invite Sharla to his place, where they would have complete privacy.

He was holding back, she knew. And although sexual frustration plagued her after the abrupt cessation of their mind-shattering kisses, she was aware of why he was holding back. Because he cared for her. Because with her it wouldn't merely be a release of his sexual urges. His emotions would be involved, and Case wasn't ready to take such a risk.

"Sorry I'm late." He strode into the lounge at that moment, still wearing his green scrub suit. "I spent the last twenty minutes with the parents of a seventeen-year-old high-school track star with compound fractures of both legs, a crushed pelvis, and a ruptured diaphragm and spleen. Motorcycle accident. Jason Fletcher and I were both working on him at the same time in the OR."

Sharla stood up. "Is he going to be all right?"

"His injuries are no longer life-threatening. We've already listed him in fair condition. But he sure as hell isn't going to be taking that college track scholarship he's been offered. With physical therapy, he'll walk again, but his championship running days are over."

"Thank heavens he won't be permanently disabled. At least he'll be able to walk."

"His parents aren't thanking anybody for anything. They're ticked off that they'll have to fork over the dough for the kid's college tuition if he loses the scholarship money. That seems to be the only thing on their minds at this point." Case clenched and unclenched his fists. His eyes were dark with anger. Sharla guessed that he'd held himself in check while talking to the boy's parents; Case was always incredibly tactful in dealing with patients' families. But he was clearly enraged by the attitude of these parents.

"Sometimes people say stupid things when they're upset, Case. Maybe they're focusing on the scholarship because they're totally overwhelmed by their son's accident."

"Says the Eternal Optimist. Don't you ever get tired of looking on the bright side, Pollyanna?"

She eyed him thoughtfully. "How long were you in surgery, Case?"

"About five hours. And I had an elective aortic aneurysm before that."

"So it's been hours since you've eaten anything. And your lunch probably consisted of a soda and a package of cookies."

"Kindly make your point," he growled.

"You're always as bad-tempered as a grizzly bear when you haven't eaten. You snarl and stomp around until—"

"I do not snarl and stomp around," he snarled as he stomped around the lounge. Sharla grinned. He came to an abrupt halt. "I don't snarl and stomp around *much*," he added rather sheepishly.

She took his arm. "Let's get something to eat."

"Where? The meat freezers in the basement? You could toss me a side of raw beef to devour."

"There's a thought." She stood on tiptoe to trace the dark circles under his pale eyes with her fingertips. "You look exhausted, Case."

"Yeah, yeah." He caught her hand and carried it to his mouth. "I don't eat right, I keep irregular hours, I should take better care of myself." He pressed his lips against her palm. "Don't come on like a wife, Sharla."

"Heaven forbid. I was speaking as a concerned friend, Case." She tried to withdraw her hand, but he tucked it in his own and headed toward the door of the lounge, giving her no choice but to trail alongside.

They nearly collided with Jason Fletcher, who was coming into the lounge. The tall, dark, and handsome orthopedic surgeon had a rakish reputation which rivaled Case's in Hospital Center lore. "I can't seem to get away from you, Flynn," Jason kidded. "It's not enough that I spent the last five hours in the OR with you, I have to literally run into you here too! Sharla, good to see you!"

"Hello, Jason," she said, smiling.

"We were just leaving," Case said, giving her hand a sharp tug.

"Nice guy, huh, Sharla?" Jason shook his head with mock disapproval. "Princely manners."

She grinned. "Princely."

Jason made no attempt to move aside and let them proceed on their way. "What costumes are you two wearing to Clare's Halloween party?" he asked jovially. "Hey, I've got it! Why don't you go in character, as Beauty and the Beast?"

"I'll bet you've been practicing that one, Jason," Sharla said dryly.

"What Halloween party?" Case demanded.

"My cousin Clare is having a Halloween party on Saturday night," Sharla explained. "Everyone is supposed to wear a costume."

"I'm going as Sherlock Holmes," Jason said.

"And I look absolutely smashing, my dear Watson," he added, lapsing into a dreadful English accent. "Your cousin doesn't stand a chance against my phony British charm, Sharla."

She gave him a hard stare. "My cousin?"

"Not Cousin Beth," Jason said hastily. "Cousin Toni. I met her in the clinic last week. Your girlfriend here is a tough cookie, Case," he complained with a devilish grin. "She warned me that if I went near her gorgeous little cousin Beth, I'd spend the next three years in traction. I think she's a part of an Armenian hit squad that protects delicious little virgins."

"Feel free to set your sights on Toni, Jason," Sharla said sweetly. "You'll get as far with her as you did with me."

"Will I?" Jason gave a lascivious leer, and Sharla laughed. Jason Fletcher was a clown, she thought. How any woman could possibly take him seriously was beyond her ken. Yet, according to hospital gossip, he was responsible for a long trail of broken hearts.

Case dropped Sharla's hand and stalked from the lounge, his posture rigid and his eyes fixed straight ahead. He did not glance back.

"What's with him?" Baffled, Jason stared at Sharla.

She shrugged. "He's hungry. We were on our way to dinner."

"He's more than hungry, honey. He's jealous." Jason chortled with delight. "His eyes were as green as the old Emerald Isle. I can't believe it. Casey Flynn, jealous because I was simply *talking* to you! Why, he and I used to pass around the phone numbers of—"

"I'd really rather not hear about your disgusting macho trade-offs, Jason."

"So what happens now?" Jason asked with interest. "Will he come back for you? Do you want me to swear to him that I never made it to first base with you, Sharla? Hell, I never even got up to bat."

"Don't worry about it, Jason. Everything will be fine." She patted his arm in a sisterly fashion. "I'm going home. It's past eight and I haven't had dinner yet."

"I'll walk you to your car," Jason said.

Case's white Lotus was gone from the physicians' parking area. "Sorry I messed up your evening," Jason said, shrugging apologetically. "I'd offer to take you to dinner myself, but I've got a cute little cookie waiting for me in the student nurses' residence."

"Cute little cookie in the student nurses' residence?" Sharla repeated with a groan. "Don't worry about me missing dinner, Jason. You've just killed my appetite."

"I know, I know. When you're not laughing in my face, I nauseate you. We went through all that the first and only time I made a pass at you. So how come you fell for Flynn, Sharla? If you'll pardon a cliché, he's cut from the same cloth as I am."

"If I believed that, I'd drive my car straight into the Potomac River." She flashed a grin. "Good-bye, Jason. I sincerely hope your cute little cookie comes to her senses and stands you up tonight." She gave him a honk and a wave as she drove out of the parking lot.

Case's temper, which had been simmering since his angry exit from the doctors' lounge, reached the boiling point as he ground the Lotus to an abrupt halt in front of Sharla's apartment building. *Sharla and Fletcher!* he thought with fury. Smiling at each other, flirting with each other, tossing off suggestive little quips! Well, they were welcome to each other! She was a man-eater and he was a womanizing piranha. The ideal match.

As for him . . . Case stalked up the staircase to the apartment Sharla shared with her cousin Beth. Sweet, pretty little Beth. Why had he been wasting his time on the older, acid-tongued cousin when there was a delectable little dish like Beth waiting in the wings?

He rang the doorbell, a predatory gleam in his eyes. Beth answered a few moments later. "Oh, hi, Case!" She greeted him with a welcoming smile.

His gaze traveled over her. She was wearing jeans and a T-shirt—and no bra. He smiled wolfishly. "Hello, Beth."

"I'm sorry, but Sharla's not back from the hospital yet."

"I know." He scowled. "She and Jason Fletcher are making eyes at each other in the doctors' lounge. Their cute little quips are enough to sour even the strongest stomach." Now why had he said that? It was hardly the way to begin a seduction.

"Jason Fletcher? The orthopedic surgeon?" Beth chuckled. "Sharla has no interest in him. I've never heard her mention his name without laughing and shaking her head and saying, 'What a jerk.'"

"They certainly seemed friendly enough to me!"

"Well, of course. They're friends. You know Sharla—she has a million friends." Beth grinned. "If she thought that you were jealous of Jason Fletcher, she'd die laughing. But I won't tell her," the girl added quickly as Case glowered at her.

"May I come in, Beth?" he asked politely. It was an effort to maintain what he hoped was a charming smile.

"Of course. I was just watching TV. Care to join me while you wait for Sharla?" Beth flopped down on the wide green sofa.

Case sat down beside her. It was time to make his move. He turned to her, his smile fixed firmly in place. "You're a beautiful girl, Beth. But I suppose you've been told that many times before."

Her cheeks grew red. "A few times," she admitted modestly. "But I've always wanted to look just like Sharla."

"Why? Taken feature by feature, you're prettier than she is," Case snapped, annoyed. "Her eyes are too big and too dark, and her mouth is too wide."

Sharla's mouth, soft and pink and tempting, and her big, black eyes flashed before his mind's eye. He felt a surge of unwelcome arousal. "She's—she's—"

"Dazzling. Exciting." Beth sighed. "Put together feature by feature, her face is so much more interesting than mine. People are always watching Sharla, she's so sparkling and lively and animated." Beth twisted a dark curl around her finger. "She has this certain magnetism, you know? She's always had it."

Case knew. He stared sightlessly at the television screen as images of Sharla tumbled through his head. "Does she ever talk about me to you?" he asked suddenly.

"Sure," Beth said blithely.

"Let me guess. She mentions my name and then laughs and shakes her head and says, 'What a jerk.'"

"Of course not!" Beth giggled. "Case"—she leaned toward him, her young face eager—"I have some exciting news. I just found out today and I haven't even told Sharla yet. Guess what?"

"What?" he asked absently. Beth's news didn't interest him in the slightest. He wanted to turn the conversation back to Sharla. What had she told her cousin about him?

"I found a roommate! One of the nurses on pediatrics is getting married and *her* roommate, an OR nurse, needs someone to share her apartment. We met and talked it over and I'm moving in next week. Of course, I'm going to miss Sharla, but I can't wait to be *really* on my own!" Beth's dark eyes glowed with excitement.

"Just be careful when you're out on your own, kid," Case said sternly. "There are a lot of guys out there who are willing and eager to take full advantage of a naive little girl like you." Good Lord, he'd come full circle, he realized grimly. He was now warning pretty young girls against the kind of man he once was. *Was.* That was the operative word. He very much feared that there wasn't a single young woman to whom he posed a threat these days. Not with the specter of Sharla continually looming in his head. Oh, yes, she'd brought the footloose Casey Flynn to his knees, all right. Here he sat, playing big brother to her nubile young cousin while *she* was out flirting with Jason Fletcher! The two of them must be having a good laugh, and the joke was all on him.

He abruptly rose to his feet. "I'm leaving," he said shortly. "If *she* thinks I'm going to sit around here waiting for her to come waltzing in after an evening with that—that—"

"Jerk?" Beth suggested.

"Jerk," Case thundered. "Well, to hell with her. I can—" He broke off in mid-sentence when he heard the key in the lock.

"Sharla's home!" Beth cried, and rushed to the door to fling it open. "Sharla, you're just in time. Case was about to leave. And speaking of leaving, I think I'll pack a bag and spend the night with Clare tonight. She might want me to help with her Halloween party plans and all." Beth scurried from the room.

"That was about as subtle as a nuclear war," Sharla said dryly.

Case glared at her. "Well, I didn't put her up to it. I was just leaving myself!"

"You haven't eaten yet. Come into the kitchen and I'll fix you an omelette. I'll make a salad too."

She walked into the kitchen, pausing only to drop her light jacket and purse onto a chair.

"You're not even surprised that I'm here!" Case said accusingly, following her.

"I saw your car parked in front of the building." She removed the eggs from the refrigerator, along with some ham, cheese, mushrooms, and green peppers. She broke the eggs into a small bowl, then began to chop the other ingredients into small pieces.

Case leaned against the counter, his arms folded against his chest, his expression petulant. "What's all this talk about your cousin Clare's Halloween party? You didn't mention it to me."

"Because I know how you hate parties. You've turned down more party invitations during the past month than most people receive in a whole year."

"I have very little free time and I don't care to waste it eating greasy finger food and making stupid small talk with people I hardly know and couldn't care less about."

Sharla put the omelette into the pan before she turned to him, her eyes alight with amusement. "And you wonder why I didn't mention Clare's party to you? In addition to eating greasy finger food and making stupid small talk, you'd have to wear a *costume*! I didn't care to brave your reaction to that!"

"It just so happens that I saw an interesting gorilla suit on sale when I went into K-Mart the other day to pick up some light bulbs and batteries. It was an adult costume, quite well made, with hair all over it and a rubber mask and—"

"You sound rather taken with it. Thank heavens you didn't know about Clare's party or you might have bought it!" Sharla laughed. "I refuse to appear at my cousin's party with a gorilla!"

"You're not going to that party without me, Sharla."

"I know." She slid the omelette from the pan onto a plate. "I never intended to go in the first place. That's why I didn't mention the party to you. I thought it would save us an argument." She gazed up at him, her dark eyes limpid. "But we seem to be having an argument anyway."

"What did you plan to do Saturday night if you weren't going to the party?" he asked challengingly.

She raised her eyebrows. "I was planning to spend Saturday night with a certain idiot named Flynn—if he wasn't performing surgery in the

Shock/Trauma Unit," she said coolly. "Any other questions?"

"What about your friend Fletcher?" Case asked bluntly, then cursed himself for mentioning the other man's name. He was doing a terrible job of playing it cool. He didn't want to quarrel with Sharla, yet he couldn't resist trying to start a fight. He was a basket case, he decided glumly. Perhaps he should have paid more attention to those psychology courses he'd found so boring and pointless in medical school.

"Jason Fletcher?" Sharla laughed and shook her head. "What a jerk! A textbook case of arrested development. He still dates teenagers." She placed the omelette, lettuce and tomato, and a half loaf of the Armenian flat bread on the table. "Let's eat, Case."

They were both hungry and concentrated on their meal. Beth came in to say good-bye, frowned at the silence, and switched on the radio for a little background noise before she left.

When he'd finished eating, Case gazed across the table at Sharla, who was pouring them each a cup of decaffeinated coffee. "That was delicious, Sharla."

She smiled at him. "I'm glad you enjoyed it."

He felt a terrible pang of guilt. "Sharla, there's something you should know. I . . . didn't come over here tonight to see you. I came over to—to make a pass at your cousin Beth," he finished bravely, and braced himself for the explosion he was sure would follow.

It didn't. "I'm sure that's what you told yourself the whole way over, Case," Sharla replied calmly.

He stared at her. "What?"

"Case, did you make a pass at Beth?"

"Well, no, but—" He broke off, frowning. "That's what I came to do."

"Mmm—hmm." Sharla stood up and began to clear the table. "So you said."

"I did *not* come here to see you!"

"No, of course not. The facts that you didn't make a pass at Beth and that you just happened to be here when I arrived are merely incidental."

Put that way, it seemed ridiculous. *He* seemed ridiculous! And Casey Flynn was not accustomed to feeling ridiculous. "Lady, if you think that you've got me so hung up on you that I'd hightail it over to your apartment to wait for you to come in after watching you make goo-goo eyes at the Hospital Center's chief rake—" He paused for a breath. "If you think that—"

"I'd be right, wouldn't I?" She gave a sultry laugh. "Have a chocolate chip cookie, Case. Beth baked them last night."

Had he been a man prone to violence, he would have taken the plate of cookies and hurled them at the wall. The thought briefly crossed his mind, but Case instantly dismissed it. Instead, he stomped out of the kitchen and headed for the apartment door. He paused to see if Sharla had followed him.

She had. She stood on the other side of the living room, still holding the cookie plate, her expression one of total exasperation. "It's fortunate that I'm a very patient woman, Case, because you can be an exhausting man. When are we ever going to get past all the denial and move ahead in this relationship? All these furious exits of yours are getting boring."

"Boring?" Case was incensed. "I threaten to walk out on you and you call it *boring*?"

"When it happens two or three times a week, yes, Case, I call it boring."

"Well, I'm sorry to have *bored* you, Sharla. It won't happen again, I assure you. When I walk through that door, it'll be for the last time. I won't be back to—to bore you again!"

She set the plate down on an end table. "I don't want you to go, Case," she said quietly.

"You don't think I can do it, do you? You don't think I can end it between us for good. You have such an inflated opinion of yourself that you believe you've got me hopelessly ensnared!"

"I'm not a spider. I haven't ensnared you in some invisible web." She gazed at him steadily, her eyes as dark as midnight pools. "You came back because you wanted to, Case."

"And I can leave whenever I want to," he said cruelly. "I'll never marry you, you know. I'll never marry anyone. So if it's marriage you're ultimately seeking, honey, you'd better tell me to get lost for good." He stared at her, a volatile and fierce anger burning in his eyes.

"I never asked you to marry me," she replied calmly. "I won't demand any more than you can give, Case."

He stared at her, charged with a fury that had no outlet. Sharla wasn't going to give him the fight he wanted, *needed*, to release the pent-up tension that had built to an intolerable level within him. "What in hell do you want from me, Sharla?" he asked roughly.

She was swamped by a tidal wave of tenderness for him. He was a complex and daunting man, but she'd fallen in love with him in spite of that—maybe because of it. She was a strong woman, and she needed a man who could cope with her strength, who wasn't intimidated by it. A man who accepted her strength, yet could make her feel intensely feminine, who could master her when she wanted, needed, to be mastered. And, for better or for worse, that was Case.

She crossed the room to him, wrapped her arms loosely around his waist, and tilted her head back to gaze up at him with her dark, dark eyes. "I don't want you to go," she said softly.

He expelled a long breath and his arms came around to hold her. "If I don't leave now, we'll be in bed within ten minutes, Sharla."

"Five," she whispered. She began to fumble with the buttons of his shirt, her fingers suddenly awkward. Her hands, always so skilled, so deft, couldn't seem to manage the simple task.

"You can thread a catheter into a vein a tenth of an inch thick," he said, "but you can't manage a few shirt buttons?" The sight of her uncharacteristic loss of dexterity touched him enormously. A ferocious wave of desire swept over him. Case felt his blood pounding in his head and his heart and his loins.

"See what a potent effect you have on me?" she whispered.

He caught her hands and lifted them to his mouth, pressing a kiss into first one palm, then the other. "I want you." His eyes glittered with the passion that was already surging within him. His hands slipped beneath her silky green-and-gray blouse, pulling it from the waistband of her slim gray skirt. "I've never wanted anyone the way I want you, Sharla. Will you believe that?"

"Yes." She framed his face with her hands. "Case," she murmured, her voice filled with all the love and desire she felt for him.

He began to undo the buttons of her blouse, one by one, maddening her with his slow precision. His fingers approached the front clasp of her bra with the same methodical care. Anticipation built and built within her, so that when he finally cupped her bare breasts with his big hands, a deep moan escaped her throat.

His thumbs skimmed over her nipples. "So hard and tight," he said huskily. "You want me, Sharla." It was a statement of fact, not a question. "Tell me, sweetheart. Tell me how much you want me. I want to hear you say the words."

And she wanted to give him those words. Loving him, she wanted to give him everything he needed, everything she had to give. She arched closer. "Oh, yes, Case. I want you. So very much." In her mind she went much further, forgoing all restraint. *I love you, Case,* she said silently. She would have liked to say the words aloud, but she knew that Case wasn't ready to hear them.

His lips covered hers with a possessive fierceness, his tongue invading the sweet, dark warmth of her mouth. His hands molded her to the long, hard length of his body, making her achingly aware of his burgeoning masculine need. Her senses began to spin as his caresses became more urgent, and uncontrollable emotions swept over her in a crashing sensual wave. She felt weak and soft and hot. Completely pliant beneath his hands, she couldn't seem to do anything but cling to him.

Case felt her weakness, and knew her surrender to be absolute. He remembered the time she had admitted her weakness for him. There was something very appealing about a strong woman like Sharla allowing herself to become so femininely vulnerable in his arms.

Her hips pressed upward, and he clenched his fingers in the rounded softness of her buttocks and held her hard against him. His mouth nibbled along her sensitive neck, and he inhaled the heady, feminine scent of her. "I feel as if I've been waiting forever to have you," he murmured.

"M-me too," she managed shakily, and he laughed with pure masculine triumph.

"Maybe I should make you plead with me to take you to bed," he said. The heat from his eyes seemed to burn incandescently into her. "Would you do it, Sharla? Would you beg me?"

He felt on the brink of a very dangerous emotion, one he'd never experienced before, one which simultaneously beckoned and threatened. She was completely exposed to him now. If he chose to be cruel, he could cut her deeply, drive her away. Or he could forge a bond between them in the most elemental, primitive, and passionate way. . . .

"Do you want me to say it?" she whispered, suddenly nervous. He could hurt her terribly if he chose. But she had to risk it. One could live a safe and sterile life in protective isolation, or one could be open and loving, despite the risk of pain. Sharla knew she would always choose the latter. She drew in a deep breath. "You know how much I want you, Case. You said the words yourself once—'We both know I can have you whenever I feel like taking you.'"

She looked small and soft, and her eyes were big and dark and deep. Case stared down, entranced by the sight of her. And then he saw the flicker of anxiety in her eyes. "I won't hurt you, Sharla," he said hoarsely, for suddenly he couldn't stand the thought that she might doubt him in any way. "If I can have you whenever I feel like taking you, then the reverse is just as true. You can have me whenever you want me."

Her arms tightened fiercely around his neck and her eyes shone with love. "I want you now, Case."

Seven

Case swept her up into his arms and carried her into her blue-and-gold bedroom. The room was quiet and dark, illuminated only by the hall light. He set her gently on her feet, letting her slide slowly along the length of his body on the way down, turning the release into a long caress. Sharla sighed softly, and he smiled at her.

"I'm crazy about you, Sharla," he admitted huskily. He gave a self-deprecating laugh. "Maybe I'm just plain crazy."

"I think you've exhibited remarkable judgment in choosing me to be crazy about." She wrapped herself around him and snuggled closer.

He held her tight, his mouth brushing the top of her silky head. "I think I have, honey." She raised her face and his lips lightly nibbled hers. "Mmm, I know I have."

Their mouths fused in a long, hot kiss. His lips moved on hers hungrily, sensuously demanding. His tongue surged audaciously into the inner warmth in a rhythm that sent scorching flicks of flame through her veins.

Sharla clung to him, moaning deeply as she sank her nails into the hard muscles of his shoulders. "Oh, Case, please. I feel like I'm going out of my mind. I've never felt this—this kind of *need* before."

"Good!" he said roughly. "I want you out of your head. Because I haven't been in my right mind since the day I met you." He was stroking away her clothes as he spoke. Swiftly, easily, the garments fell one by one as if by magic. When she finally stood nude before him, he stared at her for a long moment.

"You're exquisite, Sharla," he said quietly. His hands moved upward to cup the soft weight of her breasts. "You have beautiful breasts. So full and firm and high." His fingers toyed with the nipples, which were taut peaks of aching sensitivity. "I've been wanting to see you like this, to taste you . . ."

He eased her slowly down onto the mattress. She felt the softness of her quilted bedspread against her back as her arms came up to encircle Case's neck. His mouth fastened over the hardened tip of one breast and she shuddered as he teased it delicately with his teeth and tongue.

Her fingers clenched convulsively in his thick dark hair as she instinctively held his head close against her. "You're mine," Case said hoarsely as his hand began a slow, sensuous exploration along the curve of her waist, over the smooth flatness of her stomach, and below to the flare of her hip.

"Yes." It was the truth, and she couldn't deny it. She didn't want to deny it. Her hands moved over the sinewed strength of his back, her breathing rapid and fevered. "And you're mine," she added fiercely. He was, too, even if he hadn't yet realized it. "And—and right now you have on too many clothes."

"I guess I do." He laughed, and she savored the intimate combination of shared laughter and passion. "I suppose I'd better do something about it, if the lady insists."

"She does," she said, and watched in fascination as he removed every stitch of his clothing. "You look even better with your clothes off," she told him, her voice softly admiring. His body was all muscle and hard strength—the broad chest covered with a thick mat of wiry, dark hair, the flat stomach, the narrow hips, and the powerful thighs. He was so strong, so big . . . Her breath caught in her throat.

"Mmm, you look better with your clothes off too," he said. "Maybe I'll keep you like this all the time— naked in my bed. Any objections?"

"Just one. This is *my* bed." She was trapped in his mesmerizing gaze. "I think," she added dizzily.

He laughed at her passion-induced daze. And then her hands were tangled in the soft mat of hair on his chest. She followed the trail to his stomach where it narrowed into an arrow shape pointing downward. All rational thought fled. He was as dazed as she.

He drank deeply of her mouth, and for a long time they lay together on the bed, their bodies intertwined, kissing and holding each other. The kisses grew progressively longer and hotter and deeper. And then, slowly, their lips still clinging, they began to explore each other's bodies.

The sensations Case evoked brought a thick, fluid pleasure that rendered Sharla mindless. She luxuriated in the feelings, giving herself up to his heady male power, even as she exerted an age-old feminine magic of her own.

"Sharla, I can't wait any longer," Case said hoarsely. He'd never experienced such raw, consuming passion, such desperate urgency. He'd known desire, of course, but he'd always combined it with the inimitable Flynn style of sexual expertise. As a master technician, he was able to detach himself and objectively admire his performance. But not this time. He was too involved in the whirlpool of sensations, too caught up in Sharla's and his own responses to step outside himself.

"Yes, darling," she said throatily. "Oh, Case, please, come to me now!" Her cry was both a help-less surrender and a command. Burning with need, trembling with love, she opened herself to him completely, offering everything. She felt the warm weight of his body poised above her, felt the heat emanating from him, and then . . . he moved away from her.

"Case?" Her voice shook. If he were to leave her now . . .

"In a moment, sweetheart." He returned to her, his eyes dark, almost angry. "For the first time in my life I almost forgot about protection. Damn, if there's one thing I've been careful about from the age of fourteen, it's—"

"Fourteen?" She sat up in bed with a gasp. "You started your . . . uh, love life at fourteen?"

"It was that kind of neighborhood, that kind of school. All the guys had their first drink, their first cigarette, and their first woman by the time they entered high school. A third of the girls had to drop out because they were pregnant."

Sharla draped her arms around his neck. "But not by you. You'd seen what happened to your par-ents and were determined to avoid that trap."

He kissed her forehead. "Exactly."

"I'll never trap you, Case," she promised, then sighed. "I'm sure you've heard those words before."

He nodded. "And it's not that I don't believe them. It's just that I can't risk taking any chances. I'll always assume responsibility for taking precau-tions, Sharla." He pushed her down into the pil-lows. "Have we lost our momentum, my sweet?"

"Well, it's a little daunting to learn you've been doing this since you were fourteen." She stroked his hair. "Do you know what I was doing at four-teen? Collecting pictures of movie stars. I never even kissed a boy till I was almost seventeen."

"Yeah, well, you Armenians are a little slow. Look at your cousin Beth—a virgin at twenty-one!"

"Slow?" She gave his behind a playful smack.

"We'll see who's the slow one around here, Casey Flynn."

He laughed. "A little tip for future reference, sweetie. Fast isn't the name of the game. Just ask any sex therapist."

"I have this uncontrollable urge to smack you again, Dr. Flynn."

He caught both her hands and pinned them above her head, interlocking her fingers with his. "Let's see if we can channel those uncontrollable urges into something else, Sharla." His body came down heavily on hers, and their eyes met and held for a long, long moment.

Their gazes still locked, Case surged powerfully against her. With a wild little cry, Sharla took him deep inside her. . . .

"I love you." Sharla lay in his arms, her head in the curve of his shoulder, their legs intimately intertwined. The words slipped out. She couldn't hold them back any longer.

Case bent his head to kiss her lips lightly, lingeringly. "You love having sex with me," he corrected her, and when she opened her mouth to protest, he silenced her by kissing her again. "I feel the same, Sharla. I knew it would be good between us, but . . ." His arms tightened around her possessively. "Sweetheart, what we just had was like nothing I've ever experienced." His voice was filled with awe.

Her timing had been all wrong, Sharla conceded silently. Of course Case would attribute her feelings to their wondrously passionate union. The wave of emotion that swept over her was a thousand times deeper than passion. But she wouldn't corner him with an insistent declaration of love. He wanted to talk about the passion they had just shared. And she was more than willing to indulge him.

"It was wonderful, Case." She sighed deeply.

"Oh, more than wonderful." It had been every-thing, an explosive physical union as well as an emotional fusion, a spiritual joining of souls. But she couldn't say that to Case. She wasn't about to set herself up for the rejoinders such flowery phrases would evoke from him.

"More than wonderful," he repeated thought-fully. "There must be a higher superlative." He paused and his breath caught as he stared down at her. She was beautiful, exquisite. He adored her. No, he amended his thought at once. He adored having sex with her. That was all. But for the first time in his life Case admitted that he might be lying to himself. The realization left him reeling.

Sharla watched him, saw the sudden shadows darken his blue eyes. He was withdrawing from her, pulling back. He had found himself swept up in a sea of foreign emotions, but he wasn't about to stay in it too long.

"You said it was different for you," she said, pur-posely keeping her voice light. "I'd say that's enough of a superlative, considering the fact you've been at this for at least a quarter of a century."

A quarter of a century! he thought. A wave of depression came crashing over him. All those years, all those encounters. Names, dates, bodies blurred together into one long, forgettable sequence. His eyes connected with Sharla's. Why was he so certain that he would never forget any-thing about her? Her soft little cries, the way she had welcomed him into her, her dark velvet eyes, heavy-lidded and half-closed, as she climaxed beneath him . . .

"Case?" She slipped on top of him and nuzzled his neck. "I'm sorry. I shouldn't be so flippant."

"I don't give you much choice, do I? I don't let you be serious."

"I—I was serious when I told you I love you."

The words thundered in his head. "Were you?" A spasm of desire rippled through him. His hands glided down her body to position her to receive him. He'd never felt such violent need, such a demanding urgency. "Sharla, I want to make love to you again." He laughed harshly. "Want? That's a bit of an understatement. Hell, I *have* to have you again!"

She heard the desperation in his voice and knew that it matched what she was feeling. "I love you, Case," she cried as he filled her. And this time he didn't attempt to correct her.

"I'm not on call this weekend," Case announced three days later over a big plate of spicy rabbit *paprikash.* He and Sharla were having dinner at Csikos, a popular Hungarian restaurant in Northwest Washington. "Les Denton is covering for me. He's good—not as good as I am, of course." Case flashed an immodest grin. "But I can trust him with my patients."

Sharla glanced up from her plate of beef goulash and homemade noodles. "This is the first weekend since I've known you that you haven't put yourself at the disposal of the Shock/Trauma Unit." Supposedly, each doctor was on call only one weekend a month, but Case preferred to be constantly available to the unit, regardless of the schedule. "How did Les Denton finally win your trust?"

"Les has always been good." Case was suddenly very absorbed in breaking a roll into pieces. He did not look at Sharla as he methodically began to butter one small piece. "He's damn good. To be perfectly frank, he's as skilled as I am. I don't know why it's taken me so long to admit it."

She smiled at him. "Les may be a good trauma surgeon, but you're an inspired one, Case."

She was being loyal, Case knew. Had any other woman uttered those words, he would have immediately suspected flattery, but Sharla, as he well knew, did *not* pander to his ego. He stared at her, his food forgotten as he watched the shadows cast by the candlelight flicker across her face. He wanted her with a desire so sharp and so urgent it made him burn.

They'd made love every evening these past three days. They would undoubtedly make love tonight. He would take Sharla to her apartment and Beth would discreetly disappear for a while. When Beth returned, shortly before midnight, it would be his cue to leave. Or they would go to his apartment, and shortly before midnight Sharla would get out of bed, dress, and call for a taxi. Then he would get out of bed, dress, cancel the taxi, and drive her back to her apartment himself.

Three days and already he found it intolerable to leave her. He wanted more, more time with her. He wanted all night with her. He wanted to wake in the morning with her. Their days were so full, their schedules so crowded, it was only during their nonworking hours that they could be alone to talk and laugh and make love. And living in two separate places cut the available time to just a few hours. Case found himself resenting it mightily. He *had* to have more time with Sharla. And then he'd thought of the weekend. Three nights and two days. They could be together all that time.

And though he'd always preferred—no, insisted—that he be called into the hospital for emergencies on his weekends off, this weekend Case had taken a long look at his colleagues and realized that they were as capable, skilled, and concerned as he, that the Shock/Trauma Unit could function quite effectively without the constant presence of Casey Flynn. It was an enormous admission for him to make. For years, the Shock/Trauma Unit had been his whole life, his role as trauma surgeon the focus of his existence. Other staff members might go home to families, but to Case the unit *was* his home and family. Naturally, he wanted to believe that the place needed him more than anyone else. He *had* believed it. And he had been kidding himself, he realized. His skills, his expertise were a valued addition to the unit, but he was only a part of the whole skilled, experienced team.

The admission had jarred him into an uncomfortable acknowledgment of the emptiness awaiting a man who is totally possessed by his work. For the first time he needed something else in his life. Someone else. His eyes met and held the black velvet eyes of the woman sitting across from him. Sharla. He couldn't begin to pretend that anyone else would do.

"If you really want to go to your cousin Clare's Halloween party on Saturday." He lowered his gaze and shrugged. "I . . . uh, suppose I could go with you."

His studied indifference didn't fool her. Sharla knew him too well to misread the importance of his decision to take himself off permanent call, of actually *offering* to take her to a party, however casually he might word the offer. She leaned across the table and grasped his hands with hers. "If I had a choice between Clare's party and spending the evening alone with you, I wouldn't choose Clare's party, Case."

"No?"

"No."

He grinned. "I wouldn't choose Clare's party either." He resumed eating, feeling inordinately pleased. "So what shall we do this weekend?"

"Well, we could help Beth move . . . This is the weekend she's moving into her new apartment."

Case looked aghast. He knew enough about the Shakarian family to realize that any available Shakarian or Shakarian associate would be pressed into service. Therefore . . . he and Sharla must be unavailable. "Shay told me about this restored inn in the Catoctin Mountains in Maryland, about a ninety-minute drive from the city. We could leave Friday night and spend the whole weekend there."

Sharla's heart jumped at the thought of spending an entire weekend with Case. And at a romantic country inn . . . But she mustn't count on it. He would back out at the last minute, she was sure of that. Case wouldn't allow himself to leave the Shock/Trauma Unit for a whole weekend. Nor could he tolerate the prospect of spending a long, unbroken stretch of time in one woman's company. Not even hers. Sharla was under no illusions about her lover. "You'll go to extreme lengths—and great distances—to avoid helping Beth move," she said with a light laugh.

"I want you to spend the weekend with me, Sharla. At that inn."

Sharla was amazed when Case picked her up at seven-thirty Friday evening and loaded her suitcase into his car, alongside his own gear.

"You've been saying for the past two days that you two would never get away for the weekend," Beth whispered gleefully as Case packed the car. "Looks like you were wrong, Sharla."

"Looks can be deceiving," Sharla said dryly. "Save me a piece of that pumpkin pie, Beth. I'll be home within half an hour." She and Case said goodbye to Beth and started on their way.

"Shay said we were lucky to get a reservation so quickly," Case remarked as they drove along the Beltway, out of the city. "Usually, the inn is booked up for weeks in advance. I guess someone must've canceled and I called at just the right time." He reached for Sharla's hand and placed it on his thigh, covering it with his own. "Of course, I'm known for my extraordinary timing."

She grinned. "Mmm, I'll attest to that." She switched on the radio in time to hear the disc jockey announce the "number one song of the week." It was a song from an album that Beth played almost constantly. "I'm going to miss having Beth around," she said.

"Yeah. Sort of the way you miss a wart that's been removed from your finger."

"How dare you compare my sweet little cousin to a wart!" Sharla scowled at him, but was unable to maintain her indignation and ended up laughing. "Anyway, there are lots more where Beth came from. There seems to be a regular cousinly exodus from Racine to Washington."

"Why should you be expected to harbor them?"

"Because I have a two-bedroom apartment." She shrugged. "And I have no other commitments. The boys share a house with another guy. Clare is married, with two teenagers of her own, and Toni is practically engaged."

"Toni? The one Fletcher is planning to stalk at the party?"

"I told him he didn't stand a chance with her."

"I almost wish we'd gone to Clare's party. It might've been worth it to see Fletch make a complete fool of himself." His smile faded. "Sharla, you do know that Fletcher is off-limits to you." His hand tightened on hers. "Along with every other man."

The possessive arrogance in his tone might have angered Sharla had she not known that Casey Flynn had never been one to insist on exclusivity in a relationship. "You know what the corollary is to that, Case," she reminded him lightly. "Every other woman is off-limits to you."

"Go ahead, rub salt into the wound. Add insult to injury, you little cat." He heaved an exasperated sigh. "You know damn well that I can't see any woman but you." He cast a quick glance over at her. She was smiling.

He frowned. Damn, she really thought she had him now. He'd taken a full weekend off—his first since joining the Shock/Trauma Unit ten years ago. He had even admitted to her that no other woman interested him. *She knew that she was the only woman in his life!* Case did what any self-proclaimed, die-hard bachelor would do. He panicked.

"You're the only woman in my life *right now*," he

said quickly. "There are no commitments, no promises. I want to be honest with you, Sharla. We're not talking forever, you know."

"Oh, I know. You could decide to drop out of my life at any time. I understand perfectly, Case. And it works both ways. I can leave anytime too."

She had just described his idea of the perfect relationship, he thought. No ties. Freedom. An ever-open exit. So why did he feel like shaking her until her teeth rattled? *She could leave him at any time.* A gut-wrenching pain shot through him. But Case had learned long ago that anger was far preferable to pain. He used it as an antidote, an escape.

"Maybe we'll just turn around and skip this whole weekend farce," he said. "I'll be damned if I'm going to shell out my hard-earned money on a chick who's planning to split." He couldn't remember ever being so infuriated.

"I fully intended to pay my half," she said coolly. "I've never sponged off anyone, Case."

"Yeah? Well, it wouldn't have been sponging, Sharla. Because if we'd gone to the inn, I would've insisted on paying for the whole thing. You would've been my guest, the whole weekend would've been my treat. But since we're not going, the point is moot."

"It certainly is." She glanced at her watch. "We've been gone almost forty-five minutes. We'll be back a little later than I thought."

"What?"

"I told Beth to expect me home within half an hour. Look." She pointed to a road sign. "There's an exit a quarter mile down the road. You can get off and turn around."

"I can read the road signs!" he snapped. "You mean you told Beth to expect you home tonight?"

Sharla laughed, a little wearily. "Oh, Case, I knew we would never go away for the weekend. I'm surprised that you got this far. I've been expecting you to cancel all day."

"Oh, have you?"

"Case, I know you."

"Oh, do you?" He gripped the steering wheel until his knuckles turned white, and floored the accelerator with his foot. The Lotus roared past the exit.

"Case, you just missed—"

"Shut up!"

Sharla rolled her eyes, crossed her arms on her chest, and gave an indignant sniff. Case passed the next four exits at breakneck speed. "You're finding I'm not so predictable, aren't you, Sharla? We're heading toward the mountains."

She yawned. "We'll be back in Washington tonight. If we do make it the whole way to the inn—which I still doubt—you'll find some reason to leave in a huff. Me, the plumbing, whatever. We'll be back tonight."

The sound he made was a cross between a growl and a snarl. Sharla turned up the volume on the radio. Neither spoke a single word until Case swung the Lotus into the driveway of the stone and frame lodge. He flicked off the radio. "We're here!" he announced triumphantly. "The Shenango Inn. And *you* said we wouldn't make it."

"We're here," she conceded. "But who knows for how long? You still haven't inspected the plumbing. And you're still furious with me."

"You have the last part right. I'd like to throttle you."

"And I you." She smiled sweetly and reached for her suitcase. He promptly snatched it from her hand, then picked up his own.

"I'll carry the luggage!"

"How masterful." She hid a smile. "Will you carry it back out tonight too?"

"We are *not* leaving this inn until Sunday evening!" he thundered. "And I'm paying the entire bill, do you understand? Room, meals, everything!"

"Why should you spend your hard-earned cash

on a chick who's planning to split?" Her dark eyes were bright with amusement.

"You're laughing at me! Again!"

They were inside the inn. An oak desk was set against one wall, and an enormous stone fireplace, in which a fire crackled cheerfully, dominated another wall. The room was wood paneled and decorated with colonial antiques. The staff was dressed in colonial garb. Sharla gazed around, instantly charmed. "Oh, Case, it's lovely!" she exclaimed.

He shrugged. "It'll do, I suppose. But they'd better have indoor plumbing or I'm out of here." He caught Sharla's eye and they both laughed.

She slipped her arms around him and hugged him tight. "You're lucky I love you. Otherwise I'd have killed you miles ago."

His arms enfolded her, his lips brushed her hair. "You're the only person in the entire universe who can completely infuriate me," he said wonderingly. "And minutes later I forget why I was even angry with you." He bent his head and gazed into her black eyes. He seemed on the verge of some major insight. Which he quickly sought to escape.

"Let's check in." He pushed all disturbing thoughts and insights aside and strode to the desk to register.

Despite its rather inauspicious start, the weekend was nothing less than idyllic. They ate wonderful, home-cooked meals in the cozy, quaint dining room; they went for long walks in the woods, following the well-marked trails; they sat in front of the fireplace sipping hot spiked cider or Irish coffee and listened to music played on the inn's old-fashioned Victrola. There was long, leisurely lovemaking, in the morning and the afternoon, as well as during the dark, quiet nights. They had breakfast in bed, they had baths together in the incredibly huge claw-foot tub. And they talked.

About everything, about anything. Themselves, their families, their careers, movies, books, even politics and religion. Sometimes they teased and laughed and joked; sometimes their conversations were serious and impassioned.

When they drove back to the city on Sunday evening, Sharla knew that her love for Case had been deepened and strengthened. She wanted to believe that he felt the same. Hadn't he been attentive and loving, hadn't he seemed to enjoy every moment of their time together? He hadn't withdrawn from her, he'd drawn closer. And he'd actually stayed the entire weekend, a feat she previously wouldn't have thought him capable of.

But the cautious realist inside her reminded her that this was a man who had made a lifetime vow to avoid commitment, to escape emotional entanglements. *You're the only woman in my life right now. There are no commitments, no promises. We're not talking forever.* His words replayed themselves in her mind. She loved him, but she mustn't allow herself to depend on him. He wouldn't always be there for her. She would be a fool to delude herself into believing otherwise.

"Is Beth really gone?" Case asked hopefully as he followed Sharla into her apartment. "Are we actually going to have the place to ourselves all night?"

Sharla glanced around the extra bedroom, now devoid of Beth and her belongings. "It feels empty without her."

Case caught her around the waist and swung her up in the air. "It feels great without her!" He lowered her to her feet, then pulled her against him for a long, sweet kiss. "Did I tell you that I had a great time this weekend?"

She smiled up at him, her hands linked behind his neck. "You did mention it once or twice."

"And I didn't miss the hospital at all." He could scarcely believe it, but it was true. He'd been thoroughly absorbed in Sharla, in their relationship.

For the first time ever, his profession was simply a part, not the whole, of his life.

"Mmm, neither did I," she said.

"I'm staying with you tonight, Sharla." He couldn't envision returning to the dark solitude of his own apartment.

She snuggled closer. "I'm glad."

They stood together, holding each other tightly, savoring their closeness, their privacy, their expectations of the long, love-filled night that lay ahead. The ringing of the telephone tore through the intensely private moment, bringing it to an abrupt end.

"If that's Beth calling to say she's forgotten her hair dryer or something . . ." Case's voice trailed off into a muttered expletive.

Sharla slipped out of his arms to answer the phone. "Oh, hi, Aunt Vera!" She ignored Case's groan. "Leigh Ann wants to come to Washington and needs a place to stay?"

"No!" This from Case. "Absolutely not! Whoever she is, she's not staying here!"

Sharla shot him a stern glance and placed her fingers to her lips in a silencing gesture. Case stormed from the room. The entire apartment seemed to shake as he slammed the front door. Sharla chatted a few minutes longer with her aunt Vera. By the time she'd hung up the phone, the doorbell was ringing wildly. She walked to the door to answer it.

It was Case. "Who the hell is Leigh Ann?"

"Another cousin. She's twenty-two years old and has been working in the Racine school district office, but she wants something more exciting. She'd like to get a job on Capitol Hill."

"And so the family plans to foist her off onto good old Cousin Sharla. Do they think you're running an Armenian boardinghouse here?"

"Of course not, but—"

"Yeah, sure, I know. You're the one with the two-bedroom apartment and no commitments. Damn, we finally get rid of Beth and now we're to be stuck with Leigh Ann. Who'll come after her?"

"Probably my cousin Dana. She's—"

"That was a rhetorical question, Sharla. I wasn't expecting an answer." Case gritted his teeth. "So even if we find Leigh Ann a suitable place to live, Dana will be looming on the horizon? When will it all end?"

"Another rhetorical question? Or should I mention the twins, Elaine and Elissa, seniors at the University of Wisconsin and eager to sample life in the nation's capital?"

"There's only one thing to do." He placed his big hands on her shoulders and held her firmly in place, facing him. "Turn your apartment over to your cousins, Leigh Ann and Dana and the twins, et cetera, et cetera, and move in with me, Sharla."

Eight

Sharla stared at him, dumbstruck. "You don't mean that."

Case looked as dumbstruck as she. Clearly, he hadn't realized what he'd blurted out. She laughed with relief. "Living alone suits you, Case. You told me that you couldn't even stand living with your own twin sister when you tried it for Shay's sake."

"That was thirteen years ago. And Candy is impossible to live with. She has more eccentricities than Howard Hughes." He stared down at Sharla, his blue eyes piercing. She had to look away from the intensity of that azure gaze.

She didn't want to live with him! he thought. The first and only woman he'd ever asked to move in with him, and she didn't want to do it. The realization rankled. Suddenly, what had been merely impulsive bravado became an absolute necessity. "I want you to live with me, Sharla."

"You're not serious." Was he?

"I'm very serious. Move in with me." His gaze never wavered. "Living together makes perfect sense." His hands slipped to her waist and he pulled her close. "Didn't this weekend prove that we're compatible sharing the same living space? You squeeze the toothpaste from the bottom, just like I do. Neither of us likes to talk when we first get up in the morning, we're both relatively neat, but not compulsive about it . . . What else is there?"

She stiffened. "A lot more, Case!"

"We both have hectic schedules," he pressed on. "Living in two separate apartments cuts down our time together to just a few hours. And why pay rent in two places when each of us can pay half of one? I've listed the practical reasons, Sharla. Now, onto the personal ones." His mouth began a slow, sensual exploration of her neck. "I want to sleep with you all night, love. I like waking up in the morning with you in my arms. I want to be alone with you, in the privacy of our own place, without having to bother about cousins coming and going, midnight drives, and all that."

His hands began to knead the sensitive spot at the small of her back, then lowered slowly to cup the rounded softness of her bottom. Sharla felt excitement ripple through her with a shocking intensity. His lips nibbled at hers. "Live with me, Sharla."

"Case, I—I can't." Her head was spinning. Desire poured over her in waves. Her body knew the intense pleasure to be found with Case and craved it. His mouth, hard and strong and persuasive, closed over hers, and she went weak. She couldn't think. Love combined with passion was an unbeatable combination, and she gave up the fight and yielded to him.

He felt her surrender, knew he had only to pick her up in his arms and carry her to the bedroom to make her completely his. Or he could take her right here in the living room, on the thick beige carpet or the wide green sofa.

With a soft moan, she tore her mouth from his and buried her face in the curve of his shoulder. "Make love to me, Case." She needed him, wanted him so. She was deeply in love and yearning for a physical expression of that love. It was the only way Case would let her display the depth of her feelings for him.

He tilted her head back and kissed her cheeks, her eyelids, the tip of her nose. "Not until you agree to move in with me, love."

She opened her eyes slowly as the full import of his words struck. She placed her hands on his chest and drew back a little to give him a long, hard look. "You're using sex as a weapon!"

"Am I?" He didn't seem particularly disturbed. "Well, you know how it goes—all's fair in love and war. Or words to that effect."

"Sexual blackmail *is* a declaration of war, Flynn."

"It's a war I intend to win, Sharla." He lifted her against the hard cradle of his thighs and rubbed provocatively against her. "Say yes, Sharla."

"No! I've never had a—a live-in relationship, Case. Even the words conjure up images of rock stars and models and actresses. I'm none of those things, Case. I'm a neonatologist. I'm—I'm Armenian!"

"It's time to grow up and stop being a goody-goody." His voice was silky, soothing almost. His hands continued to work their magic, softening her body, readying her for him. "We've made love, Sharla. We've spent the weekend together. Isn't it just a bit hypocritical to sneak around for sex while maintaining an outward show of prim propriety?"

"I don't sneak around for sex! And having my own apartment is not an outward show of prim propriety!"

"You claim that you love me." His lips tantalized hers, brushing them in a series of feather-light caresses, arousing her to the point of madness, but denying her the satisfying firmness of his mouth. "If you do, prove it by moving in with me."

"The modern variation of a line that's been kicking around since Adam and Eve." She meant to sound sardonic, but her voice was high and breathless. Her eyes snapped closed as his thumb flicked over an already taut nipple. She forced them open again. "Case," she began weakly. And she was weak, alarmingly so. She loved him, and all his reasons for living together were beginning to make complete sense. Because she so desperately wanted to share his bed, his apartment, his life.

"How would I explain it to my family?" she asked as she fought the sexual magnetism that was pulling her deeper and deeper under his spell. "I couldn't lie to them, Case."

"I didn't ask you to. Tell them the truth, Sharla. You're old enough to live your own life and make your own decisions without family pressure."

Of course he wouldn't understand the particular kind of pressure a loving family could exert at any age! His parents hadn't loved him. He and his sisters had always been free agents. Sharla bit her lower lip. Could she ever explain it to him?

"Will your family disown you if you move in with me?" he asked, almost mockingly.

And if so, who needs them? She read the unspoken message in his eyes. "Of course they won't disown me! They love me!"

"Love." His laugh was sharp. "It's all an illusion, honey. A pretty word that has virtually no meaning. Lovers confuse it with sex and passion. Families confuse it with duty and pride and conformity."

"Oh, Case, you're so wrong," she said softly.

"No, sweetheart. I'm absolutely right. I venture to say that if I'd asked you to marry me and move in with me, you'd have given me quite a different answer."

Oh, Lord, she would've said yes in a second, she thought. Her face flushed and her dark eyes clouded. Case correctly interpreted her silent response. "I figured." He shrugged. "Marriage conforms to your family's expectations. They can be proud of a married woman. It's a daughter's *duty* to marry the man she lives with."

"Case," she pleaded, but he cut her off.

"I'm not the marrying kind, Sharla. I don't believe in marriage, I never have. I want more with you than an affair sandwiched in between our work and our separate apartments, but I won't marry you to get it."

She stared up at him. However much she might disagree with him, Case was being true to his convictions. No one could accuse him of hypocrisy. Had she, deep within her heart, been cherishing a secret hope that he would marry her? It seemed so, for his bald pronouncement cut her to the quick.

But it wasn't fair to blame him for her pain; he had been honest about his aversion to marriage from the start. Sharla took a long, hard look at herself and her situation. She loved Case and wanted to live with him. And her family loved her. Though they might not approve of her living with a man without the sanction of marriage, they certainly wouldn't disown her.

Case cared for her, she was certain of that. He had demonstrated it in so many ways. By cutting other women out of his life, by opening up to her, by spending an entire weekend with her. By wanting her to live with him. All firsts for him. He'd come a long way for her and now, perhaps, it was time for her to experience a first of her own. To live with her lover.

"I guess I ought to . . . practice what I preach," she said, forcing a smile. "I do love you and I do want to live with you, Case." It was as close as he was going to let her get to him, and she couldn't resist. "And my family won't turn on me if I move in with you."

Alert and still, Case watched her, his gaze never leaving her face.

"I told you that I would never demand what you couldn't give," she continued softly. "And so I won't demand marriage—now or ever. Instead I'll take what you have to offer and I'll give you my love."

He twined a shiny black strand of her hair around his finger. "Is this a roundabout way of telling me that you'll live with me, Sharla?" he asked with a wry smile.

She caught his hand and pressed her lips to his fingertips. "Very perceptive of you, Dr. Flynn."

Case felt the tension drain from him. He'd been sickeningly sure that she would refuse, and, having made the demand, he had no idea what his next course of action would have been. He broke into a wide grin and scooped her up into his arms, suddenly feeling incredibly, joyously lighthearted. "We can start moving your things to my place tonight. If we take a few things over every night this week, you'll be out of here by the weekend, when your cousin arrives."

She'd never heard him so enthusiastic. He looked boyish and eager and so happy! A rush of tears pricked her eyes. She was inordinately glad that she'd been the one to spark such happiness in him. The big idiot loved her. But how could he ever know that when he'd convinced himself that love did not exist? It was up to her to prove otherwise.

She locked her arms around his neck, her eyes soft with love. "I'll have to meet Leigh Ann's plane at the airport next Saturday," she warned.

"Fine, I'll go with you," he offered magnanimously. "And we'll take her to dinner and drive around the city and show her the sights by night. And then"—he flashed a wicked grin—"we'll dump her here and you and I will go on to my place."

"To our place," she corrected him. "And I hope you aren't too territorial, because I have lots of things that'll be competing for space in the apartment."

"There's plenty of room, Sharla. I don't have many clothes or much furniture. Bring everything you want."

"You're certainly an accommodating roommate."

"Oh, baby, am I ever accommodating!" He laughed. Then his eyes connected with hers and a sharp thrill of pure happiness spun through him. Had he been at all introspective, he might have said that this was the happiest moment of his life. But he pushed all thoughts from his mind as his mouth closed over Sharla's, and they both gave themselves up to their fiercely spiraling passion.

"She's *what*?" Candace Flynn snapped into the phone, each word stiletto sharp.

At the other end of the line her twin brother grimaced. He'd known telling Candy about Sharla wasn't going to be easy. "She moved in with me two weeks ago," he said in an undertone, glancing uneasily toward the kitchen. Sharla was in there preparing their dinner. "One of her cousins is living in her apartment now and another one is moving in."

Upon being told that Sharla's apartment was hers to sublet, Leigh Ann Shakarian had extended an immediate invitation to her cousin Dana to move in. Dana Shakarian was due to arrive within the week.

"She's been living with you for two weeks and you just happened to mention it to me now?" Candy's tone was as frigid as an arctic ice floe.

"I've been busy."

"You told Shay."

"I guess I did," he said guiltily.

"Because you knew she'd be delighted. Which she is." Candy sighed. "Case, I respect your right to do as you please, but I wish you'd told me before she moved in. Fortunately, we still have time. I'll work on the agreement tonight and have it sent to you in the morning."

"What agreement? What are you talking about, Candy?"

Another impatient sigh. "Case, I know you're not at all interested in finances, but luckily for you, I am. And thanks to me and your investment broker and your financial adviser, you're a rather rich man. You have some very lucrative stocks as well as some choice pieces of real estate in the area."

"So?" Case was getting bored with the conversation. He cast another glance toward the kitchen and appreciatively sniffed the enticing aromas drifting from it. He wanted to go to Sharla, to put his arms around her and bury his mouth in the soft curve of her neck. He wanted to watch her prepare their dinner, watch her fluid and graceful movements. Since she'd moved into the apartment two weeks ago, he'd found watching her do anything to be endlessly fascinating.

"Case, you're a sitting duck for a palimony suit." Candy's strident tones drew him from his reverie. "You're rich, you're successful, and you have a woman living with you without a signed contract specifying that what's yours is to remain yours. And *not* become hers when you two split and she's feeling vengeful and greedy."

"A palimony suit?" He laughed. "Give me a break, Candy! Sharla isn't going to try to soak me financially just because we don't have a legal contract."

"If I had a dollar for every time I've heard those words from a client who didn't have a prenuptial agreement, I'd be able to retire tomorrow. Breakups bring out the worst in people, Case. And money is the surest way to stick it to someone." Candy paused for a breath. "But you don't have to worry, because I'm going to draw up an ironclad contract for her to sign tomorrow. You'll be completely invulnerable. Not even a barracuda like me will be able to get a cent from you."

Case was aghast. "Good Lord, Candy, no! I'm not going to ask Sharla to sign some kind of document that supposedly prevents her from fleecing me. It's an insult!"

"I've seen professional, self-supporting women earning top salaries strip their husbands'—or lovers'—coffers like a school of piranha, Case.

Financial or professional status has nothing to do with it. When the breakup comes—"

"There isn't going to be a breakup, dammit!" Case wasn't aware that his voice had risen to a shout.

"Oh?" There was a long pause at Candy's end of the line. "Let me get this straight, Case. You're never going to leave this woman? And you don't anticipate her ever leaving you?" She laughed suddenly. "I can't believe you're so deluded. Poor Case! Do you intend to marry her too?"

He shifted uncomfortably. "No." He wanted to get off the phone. Talking to his sister was depressing him. And making him angry. "Candy, I have to—"

"I'll draw up that contract tonight," she interrupted briskly. "Case, I'm experienced in this area. Things are rosy in the beginning stages of a romantic relationship, but once the split occurs . . . look out! It's go-for-the-jugular time."

"It won't happen like that between Sharla and me." His gaze fell on the bright modernistic painting of angles and geometric shapes that hung on the wall. It was Sharla's painting, and it had brightened up the plain white wall considerably. Just as her assortment of odds and ends had brightened up the otherwise spartan decor of the apartment. Just as her very presence had brightened up his whole life. He tried to imagine her things gone from the apartment, tried to picture her absent from his life. He couldn't. She *belonged* here with him, to him.

"I'm just trying to help, Case." Candy's voice was soft now, almost gentle. "You're in way over your head. If you were drowning in the river, I'd do everything in my power to save you. And that's what I'm doing now, in a figurative sense."

He sighed. "Candy, I appreciate your concern, but I don't need it. And I don't need a contract to protect me from Sharla. Any more than she needs to be protected from me."

"I just got a buzz from Call Waiting, Case." Candy was all brusque attorney again. "I'll be in touch." She was off the line before he had time to draw another breath.

"Who was that?" Sharla sauntered into the room and laid her hands on his shoulders. His muscles were tense and her fingers began to knead. She bent her head to drop a kiss on his neck.

He leaned back against her, his head pillowed on her breasts. "That was my sister. Who does *not* live up to her name. There's nothing sweet about Candy."

"I guess she wasn't too happy to hear that I'm living with you," Sharla surmised.

Case turned around and pulled her down onto his lap. "It doesn't matter what she thinks, as long as you and I are happy."

"And I am." She strung a series of light kisses along his jaw. "I've never been happier, Case."

She would be happier if they were married, he thought suddenly as he held her closer. Sharla had informed her parents of her new living arrangements the day she'd moved in with him, and while they weren't exactly ecstatic, neither were they condemning. And over the past two weeks the entire Shakarian family had phoned to show support for her.

What her family *hadn't* done was suggest that Sharla have a contract drawn up for him to sign, protecting her from her lover's avaricious revenge upon their anticipated breakup. They trusted Sharla's judgment, just as Sharla trusted him. And he trusted her. Case acknowledged it for the first time. He had complete faith and trust in Sharla. She would never willingly hurt him.

Her lips touched his softly. His pulses hammered as a violent surge of desire ripped through him. He tightened his arms around her and his mouth passionately claimed hers. Her tongue sought his, luring it inside the moist warmth of her mouth. The taste, the feel, and the scent of her were driving him out of control as his need of her mounted wildly.

"How do you do it?" he asked hoarsely, staring down into her fathomless ebony eyes. "How do you drive me half-mad with just a kiss?" His hand slipped under her mint-green sweater and he found her breasts, warm and silky. And all his. He felt the lush softness, the contrasting pebble-hard tip, the rapid, erratic beat of her heart.

"You have the same effect on me," she confessed shakily. A hot sweet fire was already burning within her. Her fingers sought the buttons of his shirt, then tangled in the wiry-thick mat of hair, seeking his taut nipple. She laved it with her tongue and his heart slammed against his rib cage. "Oh, Case, I love you so."

He felt a thrill of pleasure that went far beyond the physical. His hands closed possessively over her breasts and he massaged them with erotic precision. She sighed. "You love that," he said with satisfaction. He knew exactly what she liked him to do to her and he reveled in their secrets, their intimacy. One big hand slipped beneath her skirt to stroke the silky softness of her inner thigh. He'd watched her remove her panty hose earlier, knew that she had done so because he'd once mentioned that he liked to find her accessible and ready for him during their hours alone. She was intuitively successful in pleasing him.

His hand moved higher, and she ached with anticipation. "I want you, Sharla." His voice was deep and thick and husky.

"And I want you." She gave a breathless laugh. "And I know it seems terribly pedestrian at a time like this, but what about the chicken marengo?" Her voice was as raspy with passion as his own.

"We can eat it cold. Later. In bed." He swung her up in his arms and carried her the short distance to their bedroom. "I need you, Sharla." He laid her gently on the bed and began to undress her with the utmost care.

Sharla watched him, loving his gentle ministrations, for she knew that he was not, by nature, a gentle man. He kissed her and touched her almost reverently. He made her feel feminine and delicate and . . . cherished. She studied him intently and sensed an emotion stirring within him that had never been present before.

He shed his own things with a roughness and speed that contrasted greatly with the slow and careful way he had removed her clothes. His mouth moved against hers, and with a low groan he lowered his body to hers, catching her head roughly between his hands. His fingers entwined in her hair and his eyes blazed with a hot blue flame. "You're mine, Sharla. Always." A great shudder racked the length of his body. "You have nothing to fear from me. There is no need for—" His sister's words, so coldly legal and hurtful, flashed to mind, searing him. "No need for any kind of protection and precaution between us."

His hard male desire pressed insistently against her, making her fully aware of how much he wanted her. As always, his powerful, muscled body thrilled her. She loved him and desired him, and the potent combination of love and passion thrust her headlong into a flaming sensual tempest. She wanted more and more of him, wanted to envelop and absorb him into her very being. "Please, Case," she whispered achingly, urgently, "I need you now."

He paused, and gazed into her dark velvet eyes. "Sweetheart, tonight nothing is going to come between us."

She wound her fingers into his thick hair. "Of course not, love," she crooned softly. "Nothing ever comes between us when we're together like this." It was true, she thought dizzily. When she and Case were making love, he held nothing back. Physically, at least, he permitted himself to fully express all his feelings for her.

"Something does." He frowned fiercely. "Every

time we make love. Something I've always regarded as a necessity." More than a necessity, he acknowledged silently, his lifeline to freedom. "But not tonight, Sharla."

He wasn't thinking of freedom, not freedom from Sharla. He was free *with* her, free of the old demons of pessimism and cynicism that had poisoned his life. That were still poisoning Candy's.

"Sharla, tonight I need to show you, to—to prove to you . . ." His voice trailed off. It was too difficult to put into words. He'd never felt this way before. Tonight he needed to merge with her, to create, to bind them together in the most age-old, elemental way.

Sharla sensed the desperation of his need. She wasn't sure she fully understood what he was trying to tell her until she became aware that he had not paused for the small ritual which ensured both of them freedom from possible consequences of their passion. Her eyes widened as he poised above her.

"Yes?" he whispered, seeking her assent.

She knew he would never hurt her, knew in that moment that he loved her deeply. As much as she loved him. Her body felt feverish and swollen; she ached for him. "Oh, yes, darling."

Opening herself to him, she received him with all the love and unleashed passion that blazed within her. He took her completely, driving into her with an urgency and power that made her body quake with exciting aftershocks. Wildly, violently, yet with a frenzied sweetness they'd never before experienced, they were lost to the sheer force of a rapturous primal rhythm. They spun higher and higher until both reached the pinnacle of ecstasy.

Sharla's whole body trembled with waves of hot, glowing pleasure as she was transported to the zenith of sensuous paradise. Case gave her the fire of his very life force and joined her in their own private world.

They lay together for a long time, closer than they'd ever been before. Usually they talked, even teased and laughed after they'd made love, but tonight was different. Tonight they savored their intimacy in a silence profound with their separate thoughts and discoveries. Words would have been an intrusion.

"I adore you," Case whispered at last, moments before Sharla slipped into a blissful sleep. A smile curved her lips. She knew what he was really saying. "I love you," she murmured, and snuggled closer, deeper in his arms.

The shrill ring of the telephone pierced the quiet darkness of the bedroom with the impact of a speeding bullet. Case sat up in bed, glanced at the clock, and fumbled for the bedside phone. It was four A.M. Uttering a mumbled mixture of groans and curses, he grabbed the receiver from the cradle. "Casey Flynn here . . ."

Sharla lay quietly beside him, her whole body enveloped in a delicious haze of liquid sensuality. She reached up to run her fingertips along the length of his arm from his shoulder to his wrist. She wanted him again. Her body, relaxed from a deep and contented sleep, was pliant and open and—

"She's right here, Dr. Knowlton." Case's voice lost its drowsy edge and snapped to full alertness. "Sharla, for you."

Even if she hadn't responded to Dr. Knowlton's name, she would have picked up the excitement in Case's tone. "Knowlton," he whispered to her, and her heart began to thump. Jack Knowlton would be calling her at this hour only in regard to Diane Patterson and Sharla's future patients, the unborn octuplets.

"Yes, Jack?" Sharla was aware that her hands were trembling.

"Diane has gone into labor, Sharla. I thought of

trying to stop it, but the monitor showed signs of fetal distress. It's time, Sharla."

"I'm leaving right now, Jack." She dropped the phone and leaped from the bed. She began to root through her drawers, snatching underwear from one, panty hose from another.

"Diane Patterson's gone into labor?"

Sharla nodded. "Knowlton can't prolong the pregnancy any longer with that experimental drug he's been using the past week and a half. There are signs of fetal distress. Oh, Case, this is it!" She was usually remarkably calm in medical emergencies, but this time her stomach was churning with tension. She allowed herself to express the unthinkable. "Case, what if they're too small to make it? What if we lose them all? I've promised Diane, but—"

"Diane is into her twenty-eighth week of pregnancy," Case reminded her. He was very familiar with Sharla's potential patients. They'd discussed them at length many times. "Some of them surely have a damn good shot at viability, Sharla."

She managed to dress within minutes, choosing a beige skirt and rose-colored blouse without really seeing what she was putting on. She wasn't aware that Case had climbed out of bed and was pulling on a pair of jeans and a loose-fitting gray sweatshirt until they collided in the bathroom in front of the sink. She stared at him. "Case, it's four o'clock in the morning," she felt obliged to point out to him. "You don't have to be up for a few hours yet."

"I'm driving you to the hospital," he said calmly, reaching for his toothbrush.

A warm rush of gratitude flowed through her. "That's terribly thoughtful of you, Case, but you don't have to. It's cold and rainy and it's not even dawn—"

"I'm not doing it for you, I'm doing it for me. I never had a chance to tell you all the accolades heaped upon me by Mary Margaret Aiello and her family when she went home yesterday. I figured if I drive you, I'll have a captive audience to listen to every glowing tribute."

Sharla was delighted to listen to every glowing tribute, which Case related wryly, delighted to lose herself in the steady stream of conversation he provided en route to the Hospital Center. She knew that he was fully aware of her anxiety and was deliberately diverting her, keeping her occupied until she reached the labor room, where she could go into action. She was deeply touched by his thoughtfulness, and was grateful for the convenience of the ride as well. He dropped her off at the front entrance.

"Good luck, sweetheart." He caught her hand and pulled her toward him for a swift, hard kiss. "I'm with you all the way, honey. You'll pull those babies through."

Her eyes filled suddenly with tears. "Thanks, Case." Casey Flynn didn't idly hand out professional compliments. His show of faith warmed and encouraged her. And then she rushed inside, all her thoughts with Diane Patterson and the eight babies who were about to be born. . . .

Nine

The members of the press were packed into the hospital auditorium. All three major television and radio networks, along with the cable networks, were represented by a plethora of reporters, technicians, and sound and video equipment. Reporters from newspapers and magazines, both national and international, jockeyed with each other for better seats, more information.

"There are journalists here from all over the world," Roger Davis, the designated hospital spokesman, murmured to Sharla as the two of them waited in the wings. "The switchboard has been flooded with calls, the mail room is swamped with telegrams and messages . . ." He shook his head. "I've never seen anything like this before in my entire life!"

"There's never been a set of octuplets born here before," Sharla said, and felt excitement tear through her. "There's never been a set of octuplets—with all eight babies born alive—anywhere in the entire world before!"

"I'm going to go out and issue this statement

from Don and Diane Patterson," Roger said, peering out at the sea of reporters and cameras. "Then I'll introduce you, and you can take over, Dr. Shakarian. Ever have a news conference before?" he asked nervously.

She shook her head. "But after the past thirty hours, talking to those people should be a snap."

She watched Roger walk out before the assembled group. Although she'd been on duty for the past thirty hours, she was wide awake. Bolstered by yet another surge of adrenaline, she felt as if she could tackle the next thirty without even dozing.

The Patterson octuplets had indeed been born alive, thus eliminating the first fear for them—the tragedy of stillbirth for one or more of the babies. Sharla had been present for the entire birth, which took an astonishingly rapid twenty-six minutes. The speedy birth was one of the reasons all eight had been born alive. A prolonged delivery boded ill for those siblings trapped inside for too long a time.

The babies, six girls and two boys, had been rushed into the Intensive Care Nursery under Sharla's immediate care. The trained nursery staff had begun the fight for the infants' lives the moment the newborns were placed in their hands. It was a major medical miracle that all eight had been born alive, and word went out over the airwaves within an hour of the birth. And the Hospital Center had been plunged into a media circus, with all the accompanying hoopla, just as Mel Chehovitz had predicted the day he'd asked Sharla to be the octuplets' primary care physician.

It was in that role that Sharla was introduced to the worldwide press. She walked up to the microphones, seemingly oblivious to the barrage of flashing lights in front of her. She was taking fifteen minutes away from the nursery, where her star patients were hooked up to a bewildering array of tubes and wires and flashing lights.

"They are one day old today," she said into the

mikes. Her dazzling, triumphant smile relayed all her joy, both personal and professional, in the birth and the first successful twenty-four hours. Suddenly the entire press corps began to applaud.

Case, watching on a television set in the Shock/Trauma Unit's staff lounge, understood their reaction. Sharla had that effect on people. She exuded a vibrancy, an exuberance that was catching. He smiled wryly. How had he ever hoped to remain unaffected by her when she could ignite a roomful of veteran reporters?

He listened closely, his attention focused solely on the screen as she spoke. It was the first time he'd seen her since he had dropped her off at the hospital entrance some thirty hours ago. She was wearing the same beige skirt and rose-colored blouse, and she looked tired, yet irrepressibly energetic. And she sounded upbeat as she rattled off the latest information about the Patterson babies.

The fact that six of the infants were girls was fortunate, Sharla said, as female preemies were known to be hardier than males. She felt that the three baby girls who each weighed a thousand grams were assured survival. The Intensive Care Nursery saved infants of that birth weight nearly ninety percent of the time.

Diane and her husband would have three babies to take home, Sharla mused to herself, even as she responded to a reporter's question. She'd kept her promise to the anxious young mother. But now that Diane was assured of a baby—three babies!—Sharla's goals had broadened. She'd seen all eight babies born and been awed by the sight. And she desperately wanted to save each and every one. The eight of them had been born together; they deserved to grow up together.

She told the reporters, and the world via broadcasting, about the other three baby girls who were so very small but were being stabilized by feeding tubes and temperature probes and respirators. And about the two baby boys, whose condition she described as critical, but guardedly optimistic. They were larger than the three littlest girls, but not as heavy as their three "big" sisters.

Later that day, the hospital allowed a television camera crew to film the now-famous infants through the glass window of the nursery. Sharla was seen hovering over one Isolette, moving quickly to another, always in motion, yet never appearing hurried, her demeanor one of steady, confident competence.

Sharla had an emotional visit with Diane, her husband, and her mother, and all four of them cried and laughed together. "We're naming one of the girls Sharla, after you, and one of the boys Jack, for Dr. Knowlton," Diane announced proudly.

Sharla felt a fresh flow of tears stream down her cheeks, and she hugged Diane hard. She'd never had a baby named after her, and as she stared at Baby A, as the newly named Sharla Patterson was known to the staff, a fierce wave of emotion swept over her.

The hours passed without any resemblance to the normal passage of days or routine. Sharla managed to catch a little sleep on the couch in Mel's office now and then, but nearly all of her time was spent in the nursery, anticipating crises and heading them off, dealing with abrupt changes in condition, balancing, restoring, taking necessary risks, exerting caution.

When the octuplets were three days old, she allowed herself to go home for the first time since their birth. It was nearly five in the afternoon, and she knew Case wouldn't be at the apartment. But he would be home tonight by seven and would bring dinner with him. She'd received that message from him via Beth, whom he'd collared in the cafeteria. Getting hold of anyone in the Intensive Care Nursery was almost an impossibility these past few days, as they were swamped with callers concerned about the Patterson babies' condition.

Sharla thought of her lover and was filled with intense pleasure. She couldn't wait to see him. She had so much to tell him, there was so much to talk about. She allowed herself to remember the last time they'd made love, and felt a rush of passion and tenderness. It had been so special, one of their most beautiful, memorable times together.

She showered, washed her hair, and slipped into silky cinnamon-colored Chinese-style lounging pajamas. She'd never owned such a sexy, impractical outfit until she'd received it as a thank-you gift from her cousins, Leigh Ann and Dana, for subletting her apartment to them. Apparently her young cousins felt that a woman who lived with her lover would have use for such garments.

Sharla sipped a cup of rich, strong coffee, her feet curled under her on the wide green sofa that she'd brought with her from her old apartment. She flipped through a weekly news magazine and realized that next week's issue would feature an article on the octuplets. She'd already given detailed statements to both *Time* and *Newsweek*. *People, Life*, and a host of women's magazines had already called to ask both her and Diane for interviews.

The doorbell rang, and Sharla rose with a small sigh to answer it. It was too much to hope that her peaceful solitude would last until Case came home. And any remaining hopes of peaceful solitude she might have been nourishing died at the sight of Candace Flynn standing outside her front door.

"Won't you come in, Candy?" Sharla smiled tentatively as she invited Case's twin sister inside.

Candy did not smile back. She was dressed for serious business, in an expensively tailored gray suit, brightened by a dramatic emerald-green blouse that sharply accentuated the deep green of her eyes.

"Case isn't here," Sharla said. "Would you care

for some coffee?" She felt very much like a nervous student summoned to the principal's office for some unknown offense. Candace Flynn was definitely an imposing, intimidating presence.

"No coffee, thanks." Candy seated herself on the sofa and opened her leather briefcase. "I've been following the progress of your little patients on the news. You handle yourself very well in front of the cameras, Sharla."

"Thank you." Sharla sat down at the other end of the sofa and watched Candy remove a sheaf of papers.

"Has Case mentioned the contract to you?" Candy asked, dropping all pretense of small talk. Sharla shook her head. "I thought not. The man is quite besotted at this point." Candy pinned Sharla with a coolly assessing stare. "I suppose you're aware that you're the first woman Case has ever asked to move in with him. He's a complete novice in such arrangements and it falls to me to keep his legal affairs running smoothly."

Here it comes, Sharla thought, and wasn't surprised when Candy launched into a detailed explanation of the contract she'd drawn up and would have notarized after Sharla signed it.

"What it boils down to, in essence," she said," is that you won't make any financial claims on Case after you split. You and Case need only sign for the contract to be fully and legally binding. You will sign, won't you, Sharla?" Candy asked, a challenge in her piercing green eyes.

"I assume that the reverse also holds true?" Sharla asked dryly. "That Case won't make any financial claims on *me*?" She was more amused than insulted by Candy's determined legal protection of her brother. In dealing with the difficult Flynn siblings, a sense of humor was an absolute necessity. Candy was merely demonstrating her loyalty to her brother, and Sharla knew all about family loyalty. A mischievous gleam lit her dark eyes. "A woman can't be too careful these days, you know."

"I know," Candy replied in all seriousness. "Of course you're equally protected by this contract, Sharla." She watched Sharla reach for the pen. "Er, aren't you going to read it first?"

Sharla leafed swiftly through the seven-page document. "I get the gist of it." She signed her name without a moment's hesitation.

Candy visibly relaxed. She even smiled. "I'm delighted that you're being so reasonable about this, Sharla. Frankly, I didn't know what to expect. It's a pleasure dealing with a mature, sensible woman . . . who has her own interests to protect."

Her foremost interest was in protecting her relationship with Case, Sharla thought. A legal feud with his suspicious—no, make that paranoid—twin sister would certainly be damaging.

"Did you draw up a prenuptial contract for Shay and Adam?" Sharla couldn't resist asking.

"Are you mad? Of course not! Shay had nothing when she married Adam. *He's* the one who should have had an attorney draw up an agreement, but he didn't." Candy shook her head, obviously unable to comprehend such a lack of foresight. "I don't understand him. I don't understand *them*. Shay is so—so different from me." She sighed. "I don't understand you, either Sharla. You signed the contract without even reading it, you didn't ask for legal representation for yourself. You just threw away a great opportunity to put my brother through financial hell after he kicks you out."

"I don't want to put Case through any kind of hell, Candy. No matter what happens between us."

Candy stared at her for a long moment. "You're either admirably altruistic or incredibly naive."

Sharla smiled. "Maybe a little of both," she said cheerfully.

Candy repacked her briefcase and stood up. Clearly, she did not understand Sharla's motivation, nor did she care to dwell on it. "I'll get Case's signature at another time." She gripped Sharla's hand in a firm handshake. "And I'll send you each a copy of the agreement. Best of luck with your eight little patients." Her voice warmed at the mention of the Patterson infants. "They're tough little fighters, aren't they? I hope they make it. Well, good-bye, Sharla."

Sharla walked her to the door and said her own good-bye. It was only after Candy's departure that she considered what the contract she'd signed really implied. That she and Case would break up, that there would be hurt and bitterness between them. Pain stung her, and she swiftly cast the thought away. Candy would have insisted on a similar document even if she and Case planned to be married. Which they didn't.

There was another swift, sharp jab of pain, for which Sharla scolded herself sternly. She had promised herself not to dwell on what she didn't have, and to enjoy what she *did* have. And she had a strong relationship with the man she loved. She lived with him, she shared his life. A marriage ceremony, a piece of paper, and a gold ring couldn't make that much difference in their lives. That was the argument she'd presented to her family. And maybe, someday, she would actually begin to believe it herself.

Case arrived at six-thirty with a large mushroom-and-pepperoni pizza in one hand and a box containing eight white roses in the other. "Diane Patterson is getting all the flowers," he said. "I thought the second most important woman in those babies' lives should have some flowers too."

Sharla was entranced by the un-Caselike gesture. "That's so sweet of you!" she exclaimed, throwing her arms around him. "Oh, Case, that's one of the nicest things anyone has ever done for me."

"Careful, honey, you're crushing the pizza." He awkwardly shifted the pizza box from one hand to the other. His thoughtful and romantic gesture was so un-Caselike that he wasn't sure how to deal with it himself.

She laughed and put the roses in water as he set the pizza on the table. "I'm starving!" She enthusiastically reached for a large slice of the pie. She'd eaten half of it before she realized that Case wasn't eating, hadn't even taken a piece. He was sitting across from her, staring at her with intense blue eyes.

"You're beautiful, Sharla," he said huskily.

"You think I'm beautiful even when I'm stuffing my face with pizza?" she said lightly. "You must truly be in lo—infatuated."

"Yes." He reached for her hand and interlocked his fingers with hers. He'd been thinking of her constantly during these past three days. He'd watched her on television and listened to his colleagues rave about her professional judgment and ability. And he'd been filled with a fierce pride in her and her accomplishments.

It was like nothing he'd ever experienced before. He knew he was, by nature, a competitive man. Had any other physician at the Hospital Center been singled out for international attention, he undoubtedly would have felt a shade envious, he admitted to himself. But he was genuinely thrilled for Sharla. Every complimentary word about her warmed him. He was thoroughly enjoying basking in the shadow of her sudden celebrity. It had taken a long, long time for him to see the light, but he finally had. All these feelings he had for Sharla— the pride, the faith, the trust, the need to create a life with her—all added up to something else he'd never before experienced. Love.

He was in love with Sharla, had been for weeks. But he'd been too dense to realize it. Or too stubborn to admit it. And now that he had finally realized and admitted it to himself, he was unsure how to tell Sharla. After all the disparaging remarks he'd made about love . . .

He'd caught her quick correction of the phrase

"in love" to infatuation. Perhaps this would be easier than he'd thought. "Sharla, it's true," he said. There, he'd done it. He leaned back and smiled expectantly. He'd just told her, albeit in a roundabout way, that he loved her.

"What's true?" During the long pause, Sharla had lost the train of the conversation. She was famished, and was concentrating on trying to eat her slice of pizza with her right hand, as Case had a death grip on the left one.

He could scarcely blurt out that he loved her when she was so obviously concentrating on pizza! Case thought. He stared at her, more than a little disconcerted.

She eased her hand from his. "Have some, Case." She offered him a slice of pizza. "It's really delicious. I'm so glad you stopped at Lanza's. They make the best pizza in town."

"I agree." He accepted the pizza. Yes, right now was definitely not the time to utter a passionate declaration of love. But there would be other times . . .

"I want to hear all about the Pattersons," he demanded with a smile. Sharla needed no further encouragement to launch into a detailed account of her now-famous tiny patients.

The phone began ringing before they finished the pizza, and it continued to ring steadily all evening. Family members, friends, medical colleagues—everyone who hadn't been able to get in touch with Sharla for the past three days. Case resisted the urge to rip the phone from its jack. If Sharla hadn't wanted to talk to her callers, she would've suggested disconnecting the phone herself, he reasoned.

He listened to her, he watched her, and he tried to remind himself that she did not share his own sense of urgency. She'd told him she loved him weeks ago. How was she to know that suddenly he was champing at the bit to tell her that he loved her too?

And then the phone rang for him . . .

"That was Candy," he said after he got off the phone. Sharla was in the living room, lighting jasmine-scented candles. She'd switched off all the lights.

She whirled around to face him. His jaw was clenched, his mouth a grim line. Blue sparks flared in his eyes, darkening them to a sapphire shade. She suppressed a sigh, switched the lamps back on, blew out the candles, and waited.

The storm wasn't long in coming. "Candy says you signed some damned financial contract this afternoon," he said tightly.

Clearly, he was angry. With his sister for drawing up the contract? With her for signing it? Or with both of them? Sharla swiftly assessed the situation. It was time to get on her tightrope again. "Yes, I did." She flashed a smile, hoping to coax one in response from him. "On Attorney Candace Flynn's expert advice. Protection from a possible palimony suit, you know."

Not a trace of a smile was forthcoming. "Dammit, Sharla, don't kid around. It's not funny!"

"Case, it's easier to laugh than to get angry about it. Candy was just doing what she thought was best for you. She loves you very much."

Case refused to be mollified. "Why didn't you just refuse to sign and tear the damn thing up? That's what I would have done!"

"If I'd done that, poor Candy would've had a full-fledged anxiety attack. She'd have been certain that I was plotting to stake a financial claim after you kicked me out."

"After I kicked you out?" Case was no longer displeased or angry. He was outraged.

"Candy's phrase, not mine," Sharla said quickly. "Case, I meant it as a joke."

"Some joke! You'll notice I'm not laughing, Sharla." He glared at her. "Maybe you were in league with Candy on this. Maybe you don't want *me* to have any claims on *you*. After this octuplet business and your international exposure as their neonatologist, your future is wide open. You'll be deluged with speaking offers and requests for interviews. Medical schools will want you as a prestige name on their faculty, university hospitals will offer you incredible incentive bonuses to grace their staffs. You have only to pick and choose the most attractive—and lucrative—offer."

"I don't want to leave the Hospital Center," she said succinctly. "And I'm not interested in lecturing or teaching. I want to be in the Intensive Care Nursery. And I'm not worried about you trying to gouge me financially after—" She broke off abruptly and rolled her eyes heavenward. "This conversation is beyond absurd."

"After we break up. That's what you were going to say, isn't it, Sharla? Because you intend to break up with me when you move on to more exalted career opportunities." The pain was so great, he could only bear it by exploding into fury. "Have you acquired an agent yet, Dr. Celebrity? When do you plan to be booked onto the Carson show?"

His fury was contagious. Sharla tried to count to ten; she got as far as six. She tried to summon her sense of humor, but it seemed to have evaporated. Her temper flared, then blew sky-high. "I signed the damn contract to shut Candy up and get her off my back! What do I have to do to get you to do the same?"

Case stared at her. This was a side of Sharla he had never seen before. She never shouted at him. She jollied him out of his fits of pique with her agile humor; she wryly gentled him into a more reasonable frame of mind. He opened his mouth to speak, but no words came out.

"Dealing with a Flynn takes every resource a sane person possesses, and I've had to deal with *two* of them today!" Sharla raged on. "I'm exhausted, I haven't been home in three days, and now you—" She broke off, furious. "I'm going back to the hospital. It's infinitely easier to deal with an entire nursery of premature babies than with two grown Flynns!" With that, she snatched her purse from an end table and stormed from the apartment, slamming the door behind her with all the force she could muster.

She got as far as the door of the building before she realized that she was wearing lounging pajamas. Sighing, she turned around and trudged back upstairs. Case opened the door before she had time to insert her key in the lock.

"I'm the one who always goes stalking out," he said. "Have you decided to usurp my role?"

"You're much better at it than I am. You've never stalked out in your pajamas."

"An original touch. And I give you full marks for door-slamming. I think the entire complex shook."

She cocked her head and stared up at him. "You're not angry anymore? We're not going to fight?"

"I decided I'd better shut up and get off your back. You're surprisingly ferocious when you're really riled, Sharla."

"The dark side of Sharla Shakarian." She suddenly grinned. "I'd have created quite a stir if I'd sashayed into the nursery dressed in this getup."

He surveyed her lazily. "It's a very sexy getup."

"I wore it to seduce you."

He caught both her hands and yanked her against him. "Did you?"

The moment her body impacted against the long, hard length of him, Sharla felt all the tension of the past days—and last few minutes—drain from her. It was wonderful to be able to allow herself to feel deliciously weak and soft and feminine. "Oh, Case." She closed her eyes and leaned into him, relaxing against his solid body. "I've missed you so much. Let's not waste any more time talking about stupid contracts and—"

He silenced her with a deep, lingering kiss. "Show me how much you've missed me," he demanded softly, sexily, and Sharla was only too happy to obey his ardent and impassioned command.

The month of November continued in a dizzying whirl of medical emergencies, along with the accompanying professional responsibilities and obligations. There was a crisis involving Baby E, one of the Patterson infant boys. A severe case of the dreaded acute respiratory distress syndrome attacked his immature lungs and kept Sharla at his side for hours as the baby alternately failed and rallied.

Then the smallest octuplet girl, Baby H, fell victim to the same syndrome and hovered dangerously near death for agonizing, seemingly endless days. Paradoxically, on the very day that her brother showed dramatic improvement, tiny Baby H took a definite turn for the worse. Sharla stayed with the infant all through the night, ministering to her, but not expecting her to survive till dawn.

Baby H was still clinging to life as the sun's light streaked the sky. Sharla made a vow not to leave the nursery until the baby either died or showed some signs of improvement. Three days later, Baby H— now named Holly—was still waging her tenacious struggle for survival. For the first time Sharla allowed herself to believe that the little one was going to make it after all.

Sharla and Case ate Thanksgiving dinner together in the Hospital Center cafeteria. "Turkey and all the trimmings," said Case, enthusiastically diving into his meal. "I have Thanksgiving dinner here every year. It's the one time that the cafeteria really outdoes itself."

"This is the first Thanksgiving that I haven't been back home in Racine. I've worked Christmases, but Thanksgiving was the one holiday I always made sure I spent at home." Sharla stared at the institutional whipped potatoes, stuffing, and gravy, and sighed. "No one makes apple pie like my grandmother. And my mom makes these wonderful Armenian sweet potatoes . . ."

"Armenian sweet potatoes?" Case chuckled. "They never grew sweet potatoes in Armenia, Sharla. Even I know they're a native American food."

"We just call them that. She puts marshmallows and pineapples in—" Unexpected tears filled her eyes, startling Sharla as much as Case.

"Sweetheart, you really are homesick, aren't you?" He covered her hand with his and stared at her, seeing her clearly for the first time in weeks. They'd both been so busy that their paths had hardly crossed except for those occasional urgent and tempestuous nights they'd managed to steal.

She looked pale and wan; there were dark circles under her eyes. And she was picking at her meal, unusual for a hearty eater like Sharla. He felt a sudden pang of alarm. "Sharla, are you all right?"

"Of course. I'm just indulging in a wallow of self-pity." She managed a smile to reassure him. "I'm glad we're having Thanksgiving dinner together, Case. Although I'd have preferred dinner for two by romantic candlelight instead of dinner for five hundred in the old cafeteria."

"You look exhausted," he said, studying her critically. "You need a vacation, Sharla." He smiled grimly. "And so do I. Let's make a bargain. As soon as the Patterson babies are out of danger, the two of us will go away someplace."

"It's a deal." This time her smile wasn't forced. "I feel as if I've been on an emotional roller coaster, Case. I'm up, I'm down. I'm back up again. Sometimes I feel like bursting into tears for no reason at all. And I'm so tired! I thought I could never be as tired as I was during my internship and first-year residency, but I've never felt exhaustion like this before!"

"You've had nearly three weeks of constant, intense pressure, honey. You're not getting enough sleep, you're continually driving yourself. You're a perfectionist and you're trying to do what's never been done before—send a set of octuplets home in good health. It's bound to take its toll on you."

"You're right." Sharla brightened. Talking about her unusual exhaustion and her fluctuating moods was helping her. She approached her turkey with a little more interest. "It's even taken its toll on my appetite. I'm either ravenous or nauseated."

"Sounds like a vitamin deficiency." Case frowned. "You aren't eating right, either, Sharla. No doubt you've just been grabbing junk food from the snack bar."

The conversation sparked a memory of one they'd had what seemed like ages ago. "Yeah, yeah, I'm not eating right, I'm not sleeping right. I ought to take better care of myself. You're coming on like a husband, Case." She grinned at him.

His frown deepened. "I'm concerned about you, Sharla. If I sound like a husband, then so be it."

She gaped at him. Their grueling schedules had clearly taken a toll on them both. She was losing her health, and Case was losing his sanity. "That's the first time I've ever heard you use the word *husband* without your usual shudder of revulsion."

This time he scowled. Fiercely. "Eat your dinner, Sharla," he said in reproving tones. "Every last bite of it."

"And if I don't?" she challenged saucily.

"Then I'll spoon-feed you myself, right here in front of everyone. Don't think I won't, Sharla."

She believed him. This was not the devil-may-care rake she'd originally known. This Casey Flynn was concerned about what she ate and whether she had enough rest. She smiled and scooped up a forkful of peas. He hadn't even screamed in protest when she'd compared him to his most dreaded specter, a husband. Her grandmother had an expression for times like these. "Will wonders never cease?" Sharla resisted the urge to say it aloud herself.

Jack Knowlton, Diane's doctor, stopped by the nursery the next morning to inquire about the Patterson babies' condition. "I'm thinking of sending Diane home this weekend," he told Sharla. "She's tearful about leaving the babies here, but I assured her she could visit them every day."

"Of course she can! I've already told her she's welcome to come in anytime she wants. She told me this morning that she'd be going home. We both cried." She gave a self-mocking laugh. "Lately it seems that every time *anyone* cries, I cry too. I got a lecture from Case last night," She smiled in reminiscence. "He thinks I'm suffering from a vitamin deficiency."

She expected Jack to pass off her remark as casual conversation. He did not. "Oh?" he asked interestedly. "What makes him think that?"

Sharla described her symptoms. The consuming hunger. The nausea, particularly when her stomach was empty. The incredible fatigue. Her emotional highs and lows.

Jack scrutinized her face with the intense absorption of a research scientist examining a set of crucial slides.

"What do you prescribe, Dr. Knowlton?" she asked. "A week in Bermuda? I promise I'll go in a month or two. These little critters should be well out of the woods by then."

"Sharla, the signs you've just described sound exactly like the symptoms of early pregnancy." Jack dropped his bombshell without blinking an eye. "And there's something in your face . . . certain subtle changes . . . Well, you've heard of the 'mask of pregnancy.' Is it possible, Sharla? Could you be pregnant?"

Her jaw dropped. For a second she felt so light-headed she feared she might faint. She clutched the sides of a warming table for support and found herself looking into the wide, hazel eyes of little Baby A, the newly named Sharla Patterson.

Oh, yes, she could be pregnant, she thought. And she knew the exact time she'd conceived Case's child. That magical night when he had wanted "nothing to come between them." The night when she had looked into his eyes and sensed that his lovemaking meant so much more than it ever had before. Had it also meant a child?

"Iron deficiency and vitamin B_6 deficiency, with the accompanying exhaustion and nausea, are also signs of early pregnancy," Jack continued. "When was your last period, Sharla?"

His voice reached her through a haze of shock. She tried to think, to remember. She'd been too caught up with the octuplets' struggle for survival and all the ensuing hullabaloo to give a thought to certain biological functions of her own. "About six weeks ago . . ."

"Mmm-hmm. Sharla, get yourself some iron and B_6. And get yourself to an obstetrician. I highly recommend Mac McCoy. I'd treat you myself, but I'm sure you won't be a high-risk case. For which I am very thankful." He patted her arm paternally. "I want only the best for you, Sharla. And that includes a trouble-free pregnancy and a healthy, eight-pound baby."

"Oh, Lord!" An eight-pound baby? She closed her eyes. She *was* going to faint! Thankfully the moment passed, and when she opened her eyes again, she met her tiny namesake's alert gaze.

Ten

"You look happy," Case said to Jason Fletcher as they trudged into the staff lounge after a grueling afternoon in surgery. "Or is it manic? Do you realize you've been grinning nonstop for the past four hours?"

"I have every reason to grin. Her name is Danielle, and she's—are you ready for this?—a French *au pair* girl for the Moroccan ambassador's family. She's gorgeous, Flynn. She says things like 'Ooh-la-la.' A delectable little French pastry, and tonight she's all mine." Jason's grin widened.

Case laughed. "You're incorrigible, Fletcher."

"You're not. Not anymore." Jason sighed exaggeratedly. "You sure used to be, though. Remember when we were Flynn and Fletch, the dynamic duo? Remember that New Year's Eve party when we smuggled a dozen student nurses back into their dorm at five o'clock in the morning? And then compared notes and realized that we'd—"

"I remember!" Case interrupted, laughing. "Ah, the incredible stamina of youth."

"Hey, I've still got it. I'll bet you do too. Danielle

has a friend—Michelle something—and the four of us could—"

"Forget it, Fletcher. I've lost my taste for French pastry."

Fletcher groaned. "Let me guess. You've replaced it with a craving for Armenian honey."

Case's mouth curved into a slow smile. "Yeah."

"Why don't you just marry the girl, Flynn? You sure as hell act married these days. You're disgustingly faithful. There hasn't been one wild rumor about you since you took up with Sharla."

Case shrugged. "I guess it's up to you to keep the old rumor mill running and the gossipmongers mongering, Fletch."

"And you don't even get upset when I needle you for being monogamous! Case, old pal, I recognize all the signs and symptoms. I'll be waiting for the wedding announcement, and I'll send you a toaster or a waffle iron or something. You'll probably get all excited over it too. New husbands always do." Jason shook his head mournfully. "Husbands. That's a species I'll never understand, God willing."

Case hardly heard him. Wedding announcement, he thought. Why didn't the mention of it propel him into a panicked date with Fletcher's extra French pastry? He already had the answer. Because the thought of being married to Sharla was infinitely more appealing than sexual freedom with the most willing, eager, and lusty one-night stand.

Dr. and Mrs. Casey Flynn. He visualized their names printed on their mailbox and address stickers and subscription labels. Or would it be Dr. and Dr. Flynn? Perhaps Sharla would want to continue using Shakarian professionally. Well, he had no trouble with that. He cast a wry grin at Jason, who was flirting with one of the nurses. Carry on, old buddy, he thought. Someday you'll be anticipating toasters and waffle irons, and you won't give a damn about losing your much-heralded freedom.

Sharla's face flashed before his mind's eye, and pure happiness rushed through him. He wanted to get married! It was ironic that Jason Fletcher, of all people, should bring him to the realization that marriage to Sharla was exactly what he wanted.

Case rehearsed his proposal the whole way home. Sharla would be so happy, he knew. She'd wanted to marry him all along, and had lovingly and unselfishly put her own longing for marriage aside to accommodate his hang-ups. He loved her all the more for it. And was determined to make it up to her. If she wanted a big formal wedding in Racine, with the entire Shakarian clan—Case gulped, then grinned. Why, then she'd have it.

He thought briefly of his sisters' probable reactions to his marriage plans. Shay would be thrilled; Candy undoubtedly appalled. Candy would cite all the reasons why one shouldn't marry, all the views he himself had espoused over the years. Funny how each and every one became irrelevant when he thought of marriage to Sharla. She'd changed his life in every way. She'd changed *him* in every way.

For the better, he added in acknowledgment of her love. His life had been emotionally unfulfilling, his relationships shallow. He'd been a cynical, self-centered man. If it hadn't been for Sharla, he would've lived his whole life without experiencing the rich, redemptive satisfactions of a deep and abiding love.

Smiling in the darkness, he parked his car and bounded up the stairs of the apartment building two at a time. He had it all planned. He would pull her into his arms, kiss her, and say those two immortal words "Marry me."

He fumbled with his key. His hands were shaking. He'd seen Sharla's little CRX in the lot and knew she was home, so he abandoned his fight with the lock and pressed the doorbell.

Sharla opened the door seconds later. Her smile was overly brilliant, her dark eyes overly bright.

She took a deep breath as he stepped inside and reached for her. "Case, I'm pregnant."

He stared at her, dumbstruck.

She swallowed. "Do you want me to move out?"

He was just beginning to absorb her first statement when she hit him with the second. "Move out?" he echoed blankly.

"Case, I'm not going to be a burden to you. I said I'd never demand what you can't give and I meant it. I said I'd never trap you and I meant that too." She paused for breath. She'd been rehearsing her lines since Mac McCoy, an obstetrician and good friend, had confirmed her pregnancy earlier that day. "I want this baby, and I'm happy about it. I'm also going to take full responsibility for it."

Good Lord, she was pregnant! he thought. And he could pinpoint the exact night she'd conceived his child. He stared at her as images of that passionate night were superimposed upon her. There had been many impassioned nights, before and since, but a primal force had been present that one particular night, a blinding, driving need to . . . to father her child? Had he subconsciously intended to do just that? He'd deliberately done away with any precautions because he'd wanted to . . . to what? He had never fully understood his motivations that night, but suddenly they were crystal clear. He *had* wanted to give Sharla a baby, to create a new life out of their love and bind them together forever and ever.

Sharla watched him watch her. Her heart was racing and her knees felt weak. But she would not sit down or display any sign of weakness. She was strong enough to take in stride whatever Case decided to do.

"Sharla, you have to marry me," he blurted out as emotion surged through him. The woman he loved was going to have his child! Euphoria bubbled within him.

Sharla saw the strange glitter in his eyes. She could only guess at the strain he was under. A wave of compassion washed over her. "Case, I'll never ask that of you. I—I can guess how you must feel. After all these years of avoiding marriage . . . to find yourself in the same circumstances your father did, when you've been so careful, so determined to avoid it . . ." She blinked back a rush of tears.

She would *not* resort to tears or any emotional weapon, she told herself. Case must know that he was free and she could stand alone. She needed the strength from that knowledge as well. She loved Case, but she must never permit herself to depend upon him. Not with his allergy to permanence.

"Sharla, I obviously knew what could happen that night I decided to . . . uh, risk it." It was difficult to find the right words. He'd never been adept at expressing deep emotion and he cursed himself for that lack. "We'll get married, honey. Right away."

"You . . . don't want me to leave?" She held her breath. It was more than she'd dared to hope for. "You want me to stay with you?"

"Of course! Good Lord, Sharla, you don't think I'd kick out a pregnant woman, do you? Hell, even my father, lowlife that he is, married my mother. Of course we'll get married."

Hardly the tender, loving proposal he'd wanted to make! Case fumed at himself. He was a world-class clod! He, who could speak fluently and articulately on the subject of trauma medicine in front of audiences, had just bungled the most important speech of his life.

"Case, there's no reason for you to marry me," she said carefully. She smiled at him, her first genuine smile since making her startling announcement. "We'll keep on living together, just as we've been doing."

"Sharla, there's a damn good reason for you to marry me—the child you're carrying."

"No." She shook her head, her voice firmer now. "I won't let you ruin our relationship with a shotgun marriage. We're not going to repeat your parents' mistakes."

"Sweetheart, my parents have nothing to do with you and me." He realized that now, and wondered why he hadn't put the past and all its misery behind him sooner. "It won't be a shotgun marriage, Sharla. I *want* to marry you." His voice rose a little. It was slowly dawning on him that Sharla was refusing to marry him. "Honey, I planned to propose to you tonight. I was going to ask you to marry me before you even mentioned your p-pregnancy." He stumbled over the word.

Sharla noticed. "Case, of course you weren't." She stood on tiptoe to kiss his cheek. "But you're a dear, sweet man to say it anyway." Wrapping her arms around his waist, she leaned back a little and gazed up at him. "Oh, Case, I'm so relieved that you—"

"Didn't kick you out?" He managed a grim smile. He'd better get his act together and somehow convince her that he meant what he said. "I love you, Sharla." He uttered the words for the first time. They were surprisingly easy to say. If only he'd said them weeks ago!

Her eyes brimmed with tears. "Oh, Case!" She hugged him tighter.

"If you dare to tell me that I'm a dear, sweet man for saying it, I won't be responsible for my actions." He nuzzled her neck. "It happens to be true, Sharla. I love you and I want to marry you. You have to believe that."

"I believe that you love me," she said softly, cuddling closer. "But you don't have to spin a fairy tale for me, Case. I know how you feel about marriage. You've been honest with me from the start. You're not a marrying man. You don't believe in marriage. I'll never force you to compromise your beliefs, my darling."

"Dammit, Sharla, my beliefs have changed!"

"Case, you don't have to pretend with me. Life-long beliefs don't change overnight. If we were married, you'd bitterly regret it and our relationship would be over. And I love you too much to let that happen."

"You love me too much to marry me," he said glumly. Well, he deserved it, he silently acknowledged. He really did. Anyone who'd bad-mouthed marriage as long and as vehemently as he, had no right to expect his first marriage proposal to go smoothly.

"Case, we love each other and we'll go on living together. That's all either of us needs." Sharla closed her eyes and relaxed against him. It was more than she'd hoped for.

"We need a helluva lot more, Sharla. We need to be married! You're not going to leave me and you're not going to take my baby away!"

Which she could, he realized, and panic began to set in. She was one of the most sought-after neonatologists in the country. He'd seen those offers pouring in from everywhere! She need only name her price and she could go anywhere. And their child would go with her. She was free to go and do exactly what she chose to do because he'd insisted on that freedom.

If she were his wife . . . . His arms tightened possessively around her. Then it would be a completely different story. Marriage involved ties that bound wives to their husbands, husbands to their wives—and children to their fathers. A husband's rights superseded those of a lover. He wanted all the rights of a husband, he thought desperately. He wanted every tie, emotional, legal, moral, and spiritual, every bond that marriage implied. He knew how much marriage meant to Sharla. When she married, it would be forever. He wanted that permanence in their relationship. He needed it.

"Sharla, please marry me!" Had he ever pleaded before in his life? Had he ever wanted anything as badly as he wanted to be married to her?

Sharla slipped out of his arms. He was making her nervous. She'd expected him to be angry, to hurl accusations, not to beg her to marry him. Guilt could be a powerful motivator, she knew, and she was sure that his insistence on marriage was inherently bound to his father's behavior in the same circumstances. Case despised his father, and certainly wouldn't want to see himself as less conscientious or responsible than the man he scorned as a lowlife.

"We need to lighten up the atmosphere around here," she said. She managed what she hoped was a bright smile. "I know. Let's send out for Chinese food!"

Case resisted the urge to snatch her back into his arms. He sensed her need for time and space. And though he was desperate to convince her, he knew that pushing her was not a wise course of action. For now. He remembered all the times he'd held back with her in the past and how she hadn't pushed him. How had she stood it? he wondered in despair. He was not a patient man. How was he going to stand it?

He managed not to mention marriage through their first course, shrimp-stuffed egg rolls. But during their wonton soup, he proposed again. "There's a place in Fairfax, Virginia, where we can be married within a few hours. Shay and Adam were married there. We can drive over tonight, Sharla."

"Marry in haste, repent at leisure." She sipped her soup. "Case, you'll thank me for this when you return from your guilt trip."

"Sharla, I'm not asking you to marry me because I feel guilty about the baby." His voice rose. "I'm asking you to marry me because *I love you.*"

"And I'm not taking you up on it because *I love you.* Eat your soup, Case. It's getting cold."

He tried another tack as they sampled the Peking duck. "Good Armenian girls don't have babies unless they're married, Sharla. Think what your family will say! Think of Beth. And Leigh Ann and

Dana and all those young Shakarian cousins who look up to you as a role model."

She raised her eyebrows. "I'm an adult who makes her own decisions without succumbing to family pressure, Case. And my family will love the baby and me whether I'm married or not."

"Dammit, they probably will. What's happened to families these days? Where's the sense of duty and conformity and guilt?"

She laughed and passed out the fortune cookies. He grabbed hers and pulled the printed message from the cookie. "Your fortune says 'You will marry the man who is mad about you. This weekend.' "

"It doesn't say that! Let me see it, Case."

He ripped it up. "That's exactly what it said." He proceeded to read his own fortune. "Interesting. Mine says 'You will marry a beautiful Armenian woman very soon.' You may as well give in, Sharla. You can't buck fate."

"I don't live my life according to Chinese fortune cookies, Case."

"Marry me, Sharla."

"No."

"We can't have a love child, for Pete's sake! That's for models and rock stars and Hollywood actors and actresses! We're a pair of conservative doctors. Think of the kid, Sharla!"

"I am. That's why I won't marry a man who'll regret it before the ink is dry on the license. We have to be together because we love each other, Case, not out of your misguided sense of guilt. Living together simply for the sake of a child never works. You know that. You and Candy tried to live together for Shay's sake and that didn't work out."

"That—that was different." She was besting him at every turn with his own words! Truly he had been hoisted by his own petard.

He made love to her that night with all the gentleness he could muster. He was treating her as if she were a fragile, porcelain figurine, and Sharla was gripped with a maddening combination of frustration and desperation.

"More, Case," she begged, clinging to him. Her movements were fierce and urgent. "I'm not going to break. You won't hurt me or the baby. I want you. I need you." She arched against him. "Harder. Deeper. I need to know you want me."

"Of course I want you, you little idiot. I love you," he said hoarsely.

"Show me." She felt herself being swept into a churning torrent of wild passion. He loved her with a furious intensity to which she responded with hungry abandon. She was infused with a rapture that burned through her veins like molten lava. He loved her, she exulted. It was her last coherent thought before she exploded in the fiery glow of the impassioned inferno which claimed them both.

She was reassured by the fierceness of his lovemaking. *That* could not be inspired by guilt. Replete and content, she fell asleep in his arms. Case held her, stroking her hair for a long time, listening to the steady rhythm of her soft breathing.

She hadn't regarded his proposal of marriage as a declaration of love, he thought. She'd needed physical proof of his love. Sexual proof. He sighed. And he'd set it all up himself. Congratulations, you flea-brained fool, he scorned himself. You now have exactly what you insisted you wanted. No bonds, no vows, no marriage. A lover, but not a wife. He'd kept himself just out of reach of the woman he adored, and now she was just out of his own reach.

He eased Sharla out of his arms and slipped from the bed. His gaze fell on the clock. One A.M. Impulsively, he dialed his sister's number. "Shay, did I wake you?" He didn't wait for an answer. "Sharla's pregnant," he blurted out.

Shay gasped. "Yikes!"

"And she won't marry me. She thinks that the only reason I want to marry her is because I feel guilty, that I'll feel trapped by marriage, that I'll resent her and my loss of freedom."

"Gee, I wonder where she got a crazy notion like that?"

"Yeah, I wonder." His voice deepened. "Shay, I've made such a mess of things! What am I going to do? How can I convince Sharla that I really want to marry her? I swear I was going to propose before she said one word about the baby!"

"A baby!" Shay said, delighted. "Oh, Case, you're going to be a father!"

"I'd like to be a husband first. How did Adam do it, Shay? We Flynns are a suspicious, mistrustful, cynical bunch. How did he ever convince you that he loved you and that it was permanent between you?"

"You mean you finally believe that Adam and I love each other? And that we're together permanently?"

"Yes, Shay, I finally believe it," Case said quietly. "Because now I know it's possible for people to love and stay together permanently. But, dammit, I need some help convincing Sharla that I believe in marriage and forever. Help me out, Shay."

"Well . . . She paused. "Be persistent. And inventive. And . . . creative."

"Persistent. Inventive. Creative. Hmm, this is what worked for Adam?"

She laughed. "Shall I wake him up to verify it? Case, I'm happy for you." She was suddenly serious. "I'm glad that you have Sharla. She loves you so."

"I know." He groaned. "She loves me so much that she's trying to save me from what she thinks will make me miserable—marrying her. Except it won't make me miserable. It's what I want, what I need most in this world."

"You've convinced me. Now convince Sharla."

"Persistent, inventive, creative." He fell asleep chanting the litany.

He brought her breakfast in bed the next

morning—weak tea and toast. Sharla managed to choke it down, although she was longing for a strong cup of coffee, fruit, sweet rolls, and eggs. She wasn't suffering from morning sickness, but she didn't have the heart to tell Case, who seemed to believe that an expectant mother would shudder at the sight of a hearty meal. He was being so solicitous. He braved the rainy, early morning chill and started her car, so it was warm and running for her when she was ready to drive to the hospital.

When she arrived at the nursery, she found an enormous bunch of Mylar balloons filling the supply room. Each bore a different message in a variety of brilliant colors. I LOVE YOU. MY SWEETHEART. YOU'RE MY ONE AND ONLY. And the largest, a red heart-shaped balloon, proclaimed in bold gold letters: MARRY ME.

"What's this?" Sharla asked Evelyn Foster, who was filling out an order form for Central Supply. A slow warmth suffused her cheeks. Case wouldn't carry their own private—discussion? argument?—whatever they were engaged in, to work, would he?

"Arrived at seven this morning." The nurse chuckled. "The card was addressed simply to Sharla."

Sharla blushed. And gulped. "M-me?"

Brian Cranston, the first-year resident, walked in to catch the last part of their conversation. "Unless Baby Sharla Patterson has inspired someone to propose, the only other Sharla around here is you, Dr. Shakarian. Have you set the date yet?"

"No," she said tightly. How dare Case set her up for such speculation? "Evelyn, we can't keep these balloons in here, there's no room for them. See that they're taken down to pediatrics and distributed to the children on the wards."

She donned her gown and mask and headed into the nursery. "Whew," she heard Brian say to Evelyn, "remind me never to propose via balloon. It looks like Case's proposal went over like a lead one."

"Sharla, I'm so excited! I can't wait!" Beth accosted her in the hospital cafeteria at lunchtime.

Sharla smiled at her cousin. "Can't wait for what, Beth?"

"Why, for your party, of course. Case called Clare and me this morning and told us to invite all the other cousins in the area. He said you two have a surprise to announce." Beth's dark eyes sparkled. "Oh, Sharla, you're going to announce your engagement, aren't you?"

Sharla tensed. First he had the nerve to involve her colleagues in the nursery. Now he was dragging her family into their own private . . . war. That's what it was! Case had declared war on her. And somehow she was both his opponent and victory prize.

"I've got to run, Sharla. Don't worry, Clare and I will contact everyone." Beth gave Sharla an impulsive hug. "See you at the party. 'Bye!"

Jason Fletcher caught Sharla's arm as she was leaving the cafeteria to return to the nursery. The corridor was crowded with hordes of staff members on their way to lunch. "Okay, what's it to be?" he asked. "A waffle iron or a toaster?"

"What are you talking about, Jason?"

"Your wedding present. Hey, I'll even spring for a Crockpot." He slipped his arm around her shoulder. "I'm glad you warned me against your cousin Beth, you know. You gorgeous Armenians are dangerous! I might have ended up in the same trap as poor old Case. And Sharla, about your engagement ring—make the sucker buy you a monster rock. At least five carats. You deserve it for taking on a devil like Flynn."

"Who told you that Case and I are getting married?" Sharla asked grimly.

"The man himself. He announced it to the

Shock/Trauma Unit this morning. By now the news has undoubtedly reached every department."

"Undoubtedly." The hospital grapevine was alarmingly efficient.

"Dr. Sharla Shakarian. Dr. Sharla Shakarian," The paging operator's nasal voice came over the loudspeaker of the hospital's public address system. "Please marry Dr. Casey Flynn. STAT." She repeated the message. Three times.

Sharla stopped dead. Jason burst into appreciative laughter. "What a guy, huh, Sharla? I wonder how he managed to sweet-talk old Eleanor into broadcasting that message?"

"What a guy," Sharla repeated through clenched teeth. There was laughter in the corridor as everyone reacted to Case's proposal via the paging system.

"Well," Jason said, "if the news hadn't reached every department before, it sure has now!" He was enjoying himself immensely. "Casey Flynn permanently removed from circulation! I wonder if the nurses will wear black arm bands to commemorate the lost legend?"

It was slow progress back to the nursery. Sharla was stopped on the average of every ten seconds by someone she knew. Everyone had heard Case's proposal over the PA. There were jokes, congratulations, and more jokes. By the time she finally did reach the nursery, her face hurt from smiling.

She was greeted by Diane Patterson, who was stroking Baby D's tiny naked body as the infant lay in her Isolette rigged by wires and tubes to a metal compressor, semiconductor, and pump. "I think little Diana's beginning to gain weight, don't you, Sharla?" Diane asked anxiously, and Sharla could have kissed her. She was the first person not to comment on Case's proposal since it had aired.

Diane's concern about her baby propelled Sharla back into the world of medicine. She gratefully discussed all eight infants with their mother.

The respite didn't last long. There was a steady

stream of visitors to the nursery that afternoon. Every relative, friend, and acquaintance of Sharla's in the Hospital Center came by to offer best wishes and to tease her about Case's unorthodox proposal. Only Case himself didn't put in an appearance. The man had a keen sense of self-preservation.

It wasn't until they had both arrived back at the apartment that Sharla was able to confront him with his deed. "How—how dare you?" she spluttered furiously.

He grinned. "Do you know that you're the first woman ever to say that to me? I've seen it in print a lot of times, but no one has ever been able to work it into a conversation." He pulled her into his arms and kissed her forehead. "But you did it, Sharla. Magnificently, I might add. But then, you're always magnificent."

"Will you kindly shut up!" She tried to wriggle free, but his grip merely tightened, anchoring her securely in his arms. "Case, how could you do it? Sending those balloons was bad enough, calling my cousins about a surprise party was even worse, but your—your STAT page was the most—the most—" Words failed her. She paused for a breath, searching her mind for a suitable epithet.

"Inventive proposal you've ever heard?" he suggested eagerly. "The most creative? The most persistent?"

She tore herself away from him. "Why are you doing this, Case?"

"Why am I asking you to marry me?" He gazed down at her, suddenly serious. "Because I can't picture my life without you, Sharla. Because I love you more than I ever thought it possible to love anyone."

"Because I'm pregnant. And because you'd consider yourself lower than a lowlife if you didn't marry the woman you made pregnant."

"The fact that you happen to be pregnant has

nothing to do with our marriage. I love you, Sharla."

"Case, it has everything to do with it. Otherwise you'd be content for us to live together."

"No, I wouldn't!" His eyes flashed with temper. "Dammit, why won't you believe me? Why won't you marry me?"

"You're the man who said in all seriousness that you'd rather be dead than married, Case. And I don't care to be in competition with a gravestone and a cemetery plot and--and lose!"

His anger faded as quickly as it had come. "You shouldn't have taken that to heart, Sharla. I . . . never really meant it."

"Oh, you meant it, all right. You lived your life by it."

He swept her up in his arms and carried her to an overstuffed armchair, then sat down with her in his lap. "Hasn't it occurred to you that I actually proposed the night I insisted that we do away with all precautions when we made love? I'd carefully avoided the pregnancy trap for years. That night—subconsciously, I admit—I *wanted* to be caught in it. At that point I still felt I needed an excuse to marry you, so I . . . created one."

She stroked his cheek with her fingertips. "What does a surgeon know about subconscious motivations? You slept through all your psychology courses in med school, remember?" He caught her hand and pressed his lips to her palm.

She relaxed against him. "Case, let's not argue anymore." He was kissing her neck and she felt a hot, tingling throb between her thighs.

"No, I don't want to argue either, sweetheart." He turned her in his arms and his mouth claimed hers in a deep, sweet kiss. There was no more talk of marriage for the rest of the night.

"Persistent, inventive, creative," Case mumbled under his breath the next morning as he stood in front of the mirror shaving. Sharla ducked under his arm to splash water on her face. "You'll be driving to the hospital the usual way this morning, honey? Taking Michigan Avenue?" he asked casually.

She nodded. "Why?"

"Just wondering, that's all." He didn't meet her eyes in the mirror.

"Case, there won't be any paging surprises for me today, will there?"

"No, baby. No paging surprises today."

Sharla blinked as she rounded the corner on Michigan Avenue two blocks from the hospital. She'd never paid much attention to the billboard on the right, but the sight of her name written in letters six-feet high immediately caught her eye. SHARLA, MARRY ME, the billboard insisted in eight brilliant crayon-box colors.

She nearly drove onto the sidewalk. A car horn blared. No paging surprises, he had said. But then, she hadn't asked about billboard surprises.

Mel Chehovitz hummed a tune that was suspiciously reminiscent of the wedding march when Sharla entered the nursery. "When's the big day, Sharla?" he asked jovially.

She should say "never," Sharla told herself even as she replied, "I don't know, Mel." She should begin to set the record straight at once. Even if it meant bribing Eleanor, the paging operator, to announce to the entire Hospital Center that Dr. Shakarian was *not* marrying Dr. Flynn STAT or any other time.

But she didn't. Because she didn't want to subject Case to the intense gossip her refusal would engender? Or because she secretly intended to marry him anyway? And if that was the case, why was she giving him such a hard time? Why was she making him work so hard to win her? She knew he loved her. She'd figured that out long before he knew it himself. For the first time in her life, Sharla felt hopelessly confused.

"It's so romantic!" Joyce Fusco, one of the younger nurses, exclaimed to Evelyn Foster as Sharla stepped into the nurses' station. "Oh, Dr. Shakarian! We were just talking about you and Dr. Flynn."

"Isn't everybody?" Sharla said dryly. "I take it you saw the billboard?"

"I heard about it." The young nurse sighed dreamily. "But I think his proposal in the personal column in this morning's paper can't be topped."

"The *what?*" Sharla needed to wait only a few seconds for Joyce to open the paper to the Classified Ads. The two-inch high block letters in the personal column instantly caught her eye: *Desperately seeking Sharla. Marry me. Any time. Any place. I love you. Case.*

"It even rhymes," Joyce said. "Sort of."

"I'm a regular master of iambic pentameter," Case drawled. Sharla and the young nurse whirled around to see him standing in the doorway. "Is your answer yes, Sharla? If not, I'll put Plan E into operation."

"What's Plan E?" Evelyn Foster asked with unabashed curiosity.

"Hiring a skywriter to fly over RFK Stadium during the Redskins' game on Sunday," replied Case. "And if that doesn't do it . . ." He drew two plane tickets from the inside pocket of his jacket. "Maybe this will."

"Ooh," Joyce squealed. "They're probably to Tahiti or someplace equally, excruciatingly romantic."

"Destination: Racine, Wisconsin." Case handed the tickets to Sharla. "I know you can't leave the octuplets for a long period of time yet, so I made the reservations for Christmas morning and scheduled our return trip for the next afternoon."

"You want to come home to Racine with me for Christmas?" Sharla whispered. This from the man who'd refused to meet a few of her cousins at her birthday party? "The entire family will be there, Case. And we *all* go to Grandma's for dinner on Christmas Day. Three generations of Shakarians."

"I think I'd hold out for Tahiti," advised Joyce.

"There's nowhere I'd rather be," Sharla said, "than in Racine on Christmas Day with my family—and you, Case." A rush of tears filled her eyes, making them shine like polished black diamonds. She threw her arms around him and buried her face in the starched crispness of his shirt, oblivious to the presence of the nurses, as well as Mel Chehovitz and Brian Cranston and several others in the adjoining office.

Evelyn Foster dragged young Joyce away from the area, giving the couple some much-needed privacy. Case wrapped his arms tightly around Sharla and held her close. "Does this mean you're considering my proposal?" he murmured, his lips caressing her hair.

"You can call off the skywriter." She gazed up at him with tear-bright eyes. "The answer is yes, Casey Flynn. I'll marry you."

"My darling!" He felt a sudden liquid warmth in his own eyes. "Good Lord," he gasped, incredulous. "Tears? In my eyes? I know I've changed a lot, but this is ridiculous!"

Sharla drew back a little to look up at him and laugh. "Poor Case! The atavistic macho-man has evolved into . . . the *new* man! Sensitive. Emotional. Caring."

"Does this mean I'll say things like *we're* pregnant and talk about *our* labor? That I'll sign up for parenting classes where I have to diaper a baby doll?" He feigned horror, but looked too happy to pull it off. "Am I going to be one of those guys who videotapes the birth?"

"Mmm-hmm. And invite all your friends over to watch the tape. I can't wait for Jason Fletcher's reaction."

They held each other as they laughed, their eyes

bright with happiness and love. "I love you, Sharla," Case said softly. "I'll do my best to make you happy."

She touched his cheek. "I know you will, Case. And you'll succeed. We both will. We'll have it all, each other and our baby and our careers."

This was truly the happiest moment of his life. And this time Case recognized it and savored it. And he knew that it was only one of the countless other happy times that he and Sharla would share. There might be hard times, too, but they would weather them. Together. Always together.

"You really were smart not to cave in immediately and marry me, you know," he said, a devilish gleam in his eyes. "As usual, you knew exactly how to handle me, Sharla."

"I did?"

"You knew that I don't value anything unless I have to work to get it. I guess that's why I chose trauma medicine—there's always a struggle, obstacles to overcome. You know me so well, Sharla." He slowly, sensuously traced the outline of her mouth with his thumb.

"I had no master game plan, Case," she confessed softly as her body tightened in instant response to his touch. "I've been confused and off balance the past two days. Scared, too. I wanted what was best for both of us—for all three of us—and I wasn't sure what it was."

"But you're sure now, aren't you, love?" he asked tenderly.

"Oh, yes." She flashed a sudden irrepressible grin. "I know that being married to me is going to be the best thing that ever happened to you."

"*You're* the best thing that ever happened to me." His voice was husky and his eyes were dark with emotion. "I have the three hospital chaplains—a Catholic priest, a Protestant minister, and a Jewish rabbi—on call. They'll marry us in the hospital chapel as soon as we get our license."

"All three of them?" Sharla was laughing and crying at the same time.

"I told you I intend this marriage to be permanent. Getting married in three religions ought to tie things up pretty thoroughly. Not that I've forgotten the Armenian Church. We can have another ceremony when we're in Racine over Christmas."

"The family would like that," she said, pulling his head down to her.

A rousing cheer went up from the nursery staff as they kissed.

Epilogue

Exactly one year later, Case was drinking coffee in the Shock/Trauma Unit's staff lounge when Jason Fletcher walked in and headed for the soda machine.

"Hey, Fletcher." Case motioned him over. "I've got the latest pictures right here."

"Oh, no!" Jason groaned. "Not more pictures of Shannon! I looked at four rolls of thirty-six prints each just a couple of weeks ago!"

"You haven't seen these yet. They're of Shannon's new tooth."

"Shannon's new tooth? Hey, we're talking major thrill here." Jason sauntered over to the table. "Okay, let me see them."

Case handed him a thick packet of pictures and proudly leaned over his friend's shoulder to comment on every snapshot.

"She's a cute baby," Jason admitted grudgingly. "All those dark curls. And those great big black eyes. She looks like Sharla, thank heavens, *not* like her old man."

"And she's not cute, she's *beautiful*," Case corrected him. "And she's extremely—"

"Intelligent," Jason chimed in. "I know, I know. She recognized you the moment she saw you in the delivery room. I saw it on videotape—three times. Say, who are all these babies with Shannon?" He stared at one of the pictures. "There are—" He stopped to count. "Eight of them!"

"The Patterson children," Case informed him. "Sharla has stayed in touch with Diane. We had them all over to our house last Saturday afternoon." He smiled in reminiscence. "You wouldn't believe the logistics involved in transporting eight babies from one house to another. The Pattersons have a van with wall-to-wall car seats. Needless to say, they don't get out much."

"How are the octuplets doing?" Jason asked, continuing to study the photo. "They're older than Shannon, but she's nearly as big as some of them."

"They're small but healthy. It'll take a few years, but they'll eventually catch up to their peers in size." Case reclaimed his pictures and tucked them back into his jacket pocket. "Knowlton's got a mother expecting quintuplets down on maternity now. Sharla will be the babies' primary care physician, naturally."

"Naturally," Jason said dryly. He gave a mocking laugh. "Sharla, Shannon. Shannon, Sharla. Your family's all you ever talk about these days, Case. I hate to say it, but you've become incredibly boring."

Case was undaunted. "You're just feeling defensive, Fletch, because your life is so empty and shallow and dull."

"Like hell it is! I've got a date tonight with the new OR nurse. The cute redhead with the fabulous body." Jason smiled wolfishly. "We're having dinner in her apartment. You know where *that* leads."

Case shrugged. It sounded incredibly boring. Not to mention empty, shallow, and dull. "I'm having dinner with my wife," he announced proudly.

"Then we're going to play with the baby, feed and bathe her, and put her to bed. And then . . ." He paused. His smile was as wolfish as Fletcher's. "Sharla and I have the whole night together."

"That's nothing new. You have every night together."

"Yeah," Case said with an appreciative sigh. "Every night." He stood up. "See you around, Fletch. I'm going home." And he headed for the elevators, whistling cheerfully.

THE EDITOR'S CORNER

We've got a "Super Seven" heading your way next month. First you'll get our four romances as always during the first week of the month; then on October 15, we'll have **THE SHAMROCK TRINITY** on the racks for you. With these "Super Seven" romances following up our four great LOVESWEPTs this month and coming on the heels of Sharon and Tom Curtis's remarkable **SUNSHINE AND SHADOW**, we hope we've set up a fantastic fall season of reading pleasure for you.

Leading off next month is **STILL WATERS,** LOVE-SWEPT #163, by Kathleen Creighton who made a stunning LOVESWEPT debut with **DELILAH'S WEAKNESS. STILL WATERS** is a love story that sparkles with whimsy while proving that old saying "still waters run deep." Maddy Gordon works with troubled children, using puppets in play situations to reach them. Wary and self-protective, she also uses her puppets to fend off people who dare to get too close to her. Nothing, though, can keep Zack London away from her. This forceful, sexy, loving man didn't win Olympic Gold Medals by fading when the going got tough, so he isn't about to be deterred by any obstacle Maddie can put in his path. This is a richly emotional love story that we think you'll long remember.

Barbara Boswell's **WHATEVER IT TAKES,** LOVE-SWEPT #164, works a kind of physical magic on a reader—melting her heart while taking her breath away. When feisty Kelly Malloy is teamed up against her will with irresistible hunk Brant Madison to do a story on illegal babyselling, the words and sparks fly between them. Each has secret, highly emo-

(continued)

tional reasons for being so involved in the subject they are investigating. As those secrets are gradually revealed, along with the plight of the children used in the racket, the intensity of Kelly's and Brant's growing love builds to a fever pitch. Another very special romance from Barbara Boswell!

That delightful duo Adrienne Staff and Sally Goldenbaum bring you a richly emotional, joyous romance in **KEVIN'S STORY**, LOVESWEPT #165. I'm sure many of you remember Kevin Ross who was befriended by Susan Rosten in **WHAT'S A NICE GIRL. . . ?** Kevin is now a successful businessman, seeking a model to be the spokeswoman for his product when gorgeous Suzy Keller sweeps into his life. It's love at first sight, but a love Kevin is determined to sabotage. Suzy isn't about to let that happen though . . . and she sets out to prove it in the most provocative ways possible. He may not be able to hear her passionate whispers, but he'll feel the force of her love every day, in every way!

In **LISTEN FOR THE DRUMMER**, LOVESWEPT #166, Joan Elliott Pickart will keep you chuckling while cheering on the romance of zany Brenna MacPhee and conservative Hunter Emerson. Brenna runs a pet hotel; Hunter runs a business. Brenna lives in a wildly unpredictable world; Hunter has everything in his life organized to a "T," including his wardrobe, composed exclusively of white shirts and dark suits and ties. Despite their differences he's unreasonably mad about the woman . . . especially when he discovers a need in her life as great as the one in his! Be sure not to miss this latest delight from Joan!

I've described **THE SHAMROCK TRINITY** before, but let me whet your appetite a bit more by

(continued)

reminding you that these three interrelated love stories are by Kay Hooper, Iris Johansen, and Fayrene Preston. On the back covers of the books we describe the Delaney brothers as "powerful men . . . rakes and charmers . . . they needed only love to make their lives complete." You'll learn how true those words are to your great pleasure when reading these never-to-be forgotten romances— **RAFE, THE MAVERICK** by Kay Hooper; **YORK, THE RENEGADE** by Iris Johansen; **BURKE, THE KINGPIN** by Fayrene Preston. Be sure to have your bookseller save copies of **THE SHAMROCK TRINITY** for you! We believe that **THE SHAMROCK TRINITY** continues the LOVESWEPT tradition of originality and freshness without sacrificing the beloved romance elements. We hope you'll agree and we will eagerly look forward to your response to this "first" in romance publishing. Enjoy the "Super Seven."

Warm regards,
Sincerely,

Carolyn Nichols

Carolyn Nichols
  Editor
LOVESWEPT
Bantam Books, Inc.
666 Fifth Avenue
New York, NY 10103

His love for her is madness.
Her love for him is sin.

Sunshine
and
Shadow

by Sharon and Tom Curtis

COULD THEIR EXPLOSIVE LOVE BRIDGE THE CHASM BETWEEN TWO IMPOSSIBLY DIFFERENT WORLDS?

He thought there were no surprises left in the world ... but the sudden appearance of young Amish widow Susan Peachey was astonishing—and just the shock cynical Alan Wilde needed. She was a woman from another time, innocent, yet wise in ways he scarcely understood.

Irresistibly, Susan and Alan were drawn together to explore their wildly exotic differences. And soon they would discover something far greater—a rich emotional bond that transcended both of their worlds and linked them heart-to-heart ... until their need for each other became so overwhelming that there was no turning back. But would Susan have to sacrifice all she cherished for the uncertain joy of their forbidden love?

"Look for full details on how to win an authentic Amish quilt displaying the traditional 'Sunshine and Shadow' pattern in copies of SUNSHINE AND SHADOW or on displays at participating stores. No purchase necessary. Void where prohibited by law. Sweepstakes ends December 15, 1986."

Look for SUNSHINE AND SHADOW in your bookstore or use this coupon for ordering: